"The baby is fine?"

"Oh, the baby is fine. In fact, both babies are fine," she snapped, almost maniacally now. "It's twins," she added, and then she sobbed, lifting a hand to her mouth to stop the torrent of emotion from pouring out in a large wail.

Silence cracked around them, but she barely noticed. She was shaking now, processing the truth of the scan, the reality that lay before her.

"Well, then." His voice was low and silky, as though she hadn't just told him they were going to have *two babies* in a matter of months. "That makes our decision even easier."

"What decision?" she asked, whirling around to face him.

"There is no way on earth you are leaving the country whilst pregnant with my children, so forget about returning to New Zealand."

She flinched. She hadn't expected that.

"Nor will my children be born under a cloud of illegitimacy."

Her heart almost stopped beating; his words made no sense. "I—don't— What are you saying?"

"That you must marry me—and quickly."

TWINS FOR HIS MAJESTY

CLARE CONNELLY

PRESENTS

Harlequin®
PRESENTS™

Recycling programs for this product may not exist in your area.

ISBN-13: 978-1-335-21302-0

Twins for His Majesty

Harlequin Enterprises ULC
22 Adelaide St. West, 41st Floor
Toronto, Ontario M5H 4E3, Canada
www.Harlequin.com

Printed in Lithuania

MIX
Paper | Supporting responsible forestry
FSC® C021394

Clare Connelly was raised in small-town Australia among a family of avid readers. She spent much of her childhood up a tree, Harlequin book in hand. Clare is married to her own real-life hero, and they live in a bungalow near the sea with their two children. She is frequently found staring into space—a surefire sign she is in the world of her characters. She has a penchant for French food and ice-cold champagne, and Harlequin novels continue to be her favorite-ever books. Writing for Harlequin Presents is a long-held dream. Clare can be contacted via clareconnelly.com or on her Facebook page.

Books by Clare Connelly

Harlequin Presents

Pregnant Princess in Manhattan
The Boss's Forbidden Assistant
Twelve Nights in the Prince's Bed
Pregnant Before the Proposal
Unwanted Royal Wife
Billion-Dollar Secret Between Them

The Long-Lost Cortéz Brothers

The Secret She Must Tell the Spaniard
Desert King's Forbidden Temptation

Brooding Billionaire Brothers

The Sicilian's Deal for "I Do"
Contracted and Claimed by the Boss

The Diamond Club

His Runaway Royal

Visit the Author Profile page
at Harlequin.com for more titles.

PROLOGUE

AT NINE YEARS OLD, Crown Prince Octavio de la Rosa knew certain things for sure. He knew that he was destined to one day rule the prosperous island kingdom of Castilona, that he was being groomed for this purpose every day of his life, and he knew that his mother was the most beautiful, perfect creature on Earth, whom he loved more than anything. He also knew that he hated it when his parents travelled.

'It's only two nights, dearest.' Queen Eleanora crouched down, effortlessly graceful despite the formal evening gown she wore. 'And when we come back, you can show us how much you've learned.'

Octavio pulled a face. Part of his education included mastering the piano. His mother, a gifted musician, had insisted. And though he was naturally talented, he didn't enjoy lessons, nor practising, and saw the only silver lining to his parents' absences as the reprieve it gave him from learning.

'I mean it, Tavi. No slacking off.' She winked at him though, before tousling his hair as she stood.

Octavio nodded, transferring his attention to his father, King Miguel, who was fiddling with one of the diamond cuff-links he wore. 'Be a good boy, won't you?'

he said, already distracted by the evening ahead. 'And call if you need anything.'

He nodded, hating the rush of emotion flooding his chest.

'Okay, bye.' He tried to sound casual and relaxed.

But his mother saw. She understood. She reached down and squeezed his hand in hers. 'Two nights, my love. Don't forget…' She trailed off, waiting for Octavio to finish the sentence.

'We'll always share the stars.' He repeated the words he'd learned by rote when he was very young and would weep whenever his mother had to leave the country. She had taught him to look out at the stars and know that she was doing the same, that they would always be connected by the heavens.

The phrase did make him feel calmer. He watched as his parents walked out of the elegant gallery, his father's arm wrapped around his mother's waist, their heads bent close together as they began to converse privately, a bubble forming around them indicating how happy and in love they were.

Octavio watched them until they were out of sight, and he would always be glad for that, because that was the very last time he saw his parents. Within days, they would be dead, and his life altered for ever. Soon, Prince Octavio de la Rosa would be utterly, completely alone.

CHAPTER ONE

Nineteen years later

FROM THESE PARTICULAR windows in the prestigious Clínica San Carlos, King Octavio de la Rosa had an unimpeded view of his palace. The place that defined who he was in life—a king of this prosperous Mediterranean island country. He stared across at the palace now, the sky a jet-black. Even the stars were blanked out by low cloud cover, giving the impression the heavens were utterly bereft of light, the darkness almost bleak enough to match his mood.

Grief flooded him. Grief, for his uncle Rodrigo had just died and with him, the last touchstone to his life *before*. Before his parents had been killed and he'd been orphaned, before his life had been turned upside down. He felt it deeply, but there was also a dark anger, so intense it burned through him, alongside frustration, despair and a cloying sense of being truly alone in the world.

In reality, he wasn't.

He was rarely alone—as the King, that wasn't possible. But Rodrigo was different. Rodrigo had been a last link to his parents. The man his mother had always joked she might have married if she'd met him first had died, and Octavio had been powerless to save him. Maybe if he'd known about Rodrigo's ill health sooner?

A noise startled Octavio out of his reverie. He glanced up, on autopilot, to see one of the hospital's cleaners stepping into the luxurious suite he'd been appointed since arriving at the facility. He'd seen her before and noticed her. Even in his state of grief, he couldn't fail to notice her. She was beautiful, but it was more than that. She was graceful, like a ballerina, and there was a wistfulness in her gestures that couldn't help but convey itself.

The *clínica* was the last word in medical excellence, but it also shared some hallmarks with a five-star hotel—there were several suites such as this made available for guests of patients. For Octavio, the biggest and best had been reserved, allowing him to spend days at a time sitting vigil by his uncle's bedside.

Not that it had made a difference.

His stomach churned, impotent fury at his inability to help Rodrigo a slick of regret deep in his chest.

The woman busied herself clearing rubbish, keeping her head bent, evidently trained as his palace staff was, to exist without being seen.

It had never bothered him before. He'd been surrounded by staff all his life and had learned to live with the constant intrusion, but now, something about her self-effacing attempt to fade into the background was galling to him.

He attributed the sensation to his grief, to the shock of having sat at his uncle's bed not one hour earlier as the machines began to beep in that awful way, a flatline appearing on the equipment.

Soon he'd return to the palace, but he needed a little longer to process his loss.

To work out what he'd do next.

His uncle had died, but it had been preventable. The truth was, one uncle had all but killed the other, and Octavio had to work out how to deal with that.

The woman was lifting glasses now, stacking them on a tray, her fingers so delicate, even when they were capable. He stared unashamedly, as one might watch a performance. Her uniform was dark blue, a dress that fell to her knees and cinched in at the waist, with buttons up to her throat. Her neck was elegant, swan-like, the alabaster colour of her skin revealed by the way her long blonde hair had been swept up into a ponytail. If she wore make-up, it was minimal. Her face was clear, her eyes wide set and a striking shade of green. As if his ruminating on their colour had somehow conveyed itself to the woman, she glanced across at him then, her cheeks flushing pink when their eyes connected. Her lips parted on a quick exhalation of breath, and she looked away once more, turning her back on him.

Frustration, anger, irritation grew.

Suddenly, he didn't want her to fade into the background. He didn't want her to clear his plates and glasses and act as though she wasn't there.

'What is your name?' His voice was gruff from disuse. Even as the hospital director, an efficient, impressive woman named Lola Garcia, had gently explained the procedures from this point onwards, he'd barely spoken a word.

The woman's shoulders squared as she turned back to face him, and there was a caution in her features that should have served as a warning. He wasn't himself. He wasn't remotely like himself. Famed for his control—a control that had been etched from the fires of his life— he was disciplined at all times.

Only, he didn't feel disciplined right now.

His veins were coursing with emotions he couldn't control, with a need for something he couldn't explain.

And this woman was in the firing line.

'I asked for your name.'

She blinked quickly, her lips, full and pink, quirking down a little in one corner. 'Phoebe.' Her voice was soft, like her hair.

'Phoebe what?'

'Phoebe, Your Majesty.' She grimaced in apology.

The dark emotions in his gut twisted. He didn't want to be 'Your Majesty' in that moment. How different might his life have been had he not been born royal? If his parents hadn't been travelling on behalf of the kingdom, if his uncle Mauricio hadn't desperately sought the power of the throne? How different might it all have been?

'I meant to ask for your full name.'

'Oh, right.' Her tongue darted out, licking her lower lip. His veins pulsed with unexpected and not entirely unwelcome heat. 'Phoebe James.' Her words were lightly accented. Where was she from? What brought her to Castilona? In a fog of grief, he fixated on this woman, on the distraction she might provide.

'Take a seat.' He gestured to the chairs opposite, aware that he had no right to ask it of her, aware that she might feel pressured to agree because of who he was. He softened the request by muttering, 'If you have time.'

She hesitated and he immediately regretted adding the second statement. However, a moment later, she glided towards the armchair, pressing her hand into the back of it. She didn't sit, but she moved closer to him. He caught a hint of her fragrance, vanilla and strawberries, reminding him of summer fields.

'Did you need something, sir?'

Did he?

Yes. But what?

He knew only that he didn't want her to leave. Perhaps he was hiding from reality, avoiding his return to the palace as long as possible. Whatever the reason, it changed nothing. He was here and so was she.

'My uncle just died.'

Her eyes widened and her skin paled. 'I'm so sorry. I should leave. I didn't know, or I would never have intruded on your privacy at this time. My condolences, Your Majesty.'

She spoke quickly, the words tripping over themselves, and her sympathy was so obviously genuine that it pulled at something deep in his chest. If he allowed it, her words could weaken him, could erode his outer shell to reveal the grief and desolation deep at his core. He straightened, infusing his spine with steel, showing strength even when he didn't feel it, as was his way. As had been expected of him since his parents had died.

'It was expected.'

She hesitated, not leaving, not moving, just standing there like a deer in headlights. Then she exhaled quickly, so he was conscious of the way her body moved with the action of breathing, her breasts shifting beneath the dark blue dress.

'That doesn't make it any easier, in my experience.'

'Do you have experience with this?' Or did she mean working at the *clínica*? She must see such loss all the time. Except that wasn't what she'd meant, he was sure of it. Her teeth pressed into her lower lip, and her eyes turned a stormy green, like the ocean far, far out in its deepest parts.

'Yes, sir. And I don't think you can ever really prepare for the loss of someone you love. Nor do I think you ever fully recover.'

Fascinating. He knew her words were true—he lived them every day. There was an emptiness at his core that had been created on the day of his parents' death, an emptiness he had no hope of filling. Then again, perhaps that had as much to do with what happened to him after his parents' death as their actual loss itself. Whatever the reason, he'd spent his adult life avoiding anything like emotional dependency. Soon he would marry the Princess his parents had chosen for him, but that was an arranged marriage, without any kind of personal connection—it was a step he would take for the good of the country. He had no interest in exposing himself to any kind of loss ever again: he would be a far more effective ruler that way.

'Anyway...' Her voice trailed off a little. His eyes slammed back to her, a frown etched on his face. He reached for his tie and unfastened it, removing it completely before flicking open the button at his throat to reveal the column of his neck. Her eyes dropped betrayingly to the gesture; her cheeks flushed pink again. 'I should leave.'

'Stay.' There was command in his tone now and he

didn't care. If she'd wanted to go, she would have done so by now. Ordinarily, he wouldn't have cared, because Octavio was not a man who needed anyone else in his life, even temporarily. But tonight, grief had weakened him, temporarily, and to himself he admitted that this woman choosing to remain with him carried more weight than he welcomed.

'Why?'

It was a whispered plea, a request for truth, and so he spoke the truth that was at his core in that moment.

'Because I don't want to be alone right now.'

She hesitated. 'Is there someone I can call for you?'

No one. He was alone. His gut churned. It was how he wanted it, how it had to be, and yet the creeping sense of isolation spread through him, turning his veins to ice. Of course, there was always Xiomara, the cousin with whom he was close, but even his relationship with her was complicated, and at times tainted by the fact that her father had been, in Octavio's eyes, responsible for their uncle Rodrigo's death. He wouldn't put Xiomara in the position of coming here, now.

'No.'

A soft sigh. 'Can I do something for you, sir? Would you like a tea? Coffee? Something stronger?'

His lips twisted. 'The latter.'

'Of course, Your Majesty.'

'Don't do that.'

She blinked, surprised. And no wonder. He was acting out of character yet he couldn't stop himself.

'Just—call me Octavio.'

'I'm sorry, sir, I really can't.'

'Why not?'

'My job—it's against protocol.'

A wry grimace tilted his lips. 'Who is going to know?'

'Well,' she prevaricated. 'No one, I suppose. But I—'

He waited for her to elaborate. 'I am asking you to treat me like a man, not a king. When I leave here and return there—' he nodded towards the palace, glistening like a beacon, calling to him '—I will be Your Majesty again. But now, I am just a man who is grieving his uncle.' Grieving his parents, his family, all of it. 'Treat me like a man.'

She moved towards the kitchen and removed a glass from the cabinet. He stood, striding across to her. 'Join me.'

Again, those eyes changed colour, to almost an emerald green. Fascinating. Her lashes were long and dark, curling and soft.

'Do you mind if I make an observation?'

One single brow lifted.

'You do not act like any man I've ever met. Treating you like one would be…difficult.'

'In what ways do I differ?'

'Seriously?' A small laugh escaped then but she stifled it, glancing at him with that frustratingly deferential expression of apology.

'Yes, I am serious.'

'Well…' She looked around, lost for words. 'You're… just very regal.'

'What does that mean?'

'It means that you're clearly used to giving commands and to having them obeyed.'

'Is that a bad thing?'

'Not at all. But it's not a "normal guy" thing.'

'I only became King two weeks ago,' he pointed out.

'But you were raised to be King, weren't you?'

He was raised to be King, yes. Raised by a man who hated him, raised by a man who hired a succession of nannies to do the actual caregiving—though he used that term loosely. The only prerequisite for his nannies' hiring, from what Octavio could tell, was that they be ice-cold, and cruel to boot.

He dipped his head forward.

'And when you walk out of this hospital, you'll return to the palace, where everyone will refer to you as "Your Majesty"?'

'And I will act as though I am not feeling this,' he said, pressing to his chest, indicating his grief. 'Because that is what is expected of me there.'

'But here, with me, you can be honest,' she murmured, eyes wide, as if articulating that thought gave it more power.

'Yes.'

'Okay.' She hesitated. 'Octavio.'

His name on her lips was different; she imbued the syllables with the softness that was inherent to her, taking a name that was, by its nature and design, a symbol of strength and making it somehow more human. Just as he wished to be.

But it was more than just a softening of his name, it was the forging of a connection. She addressed him like a man and he felt it—not normal, exactly, but powerfully aware of something between them that was transcending his rank, his title, even his grief. Or perhaps it was because of his grief? Perhaps in such moments, where awareness of death was at a peak, people were wired to seek expressions of life. He wanted to feel alive, and there was something about Phoebe that caused his blood to hum.

'Tell me about your uncle,' she invited, pouring a Scotch and sliding it across to him. He ignored the drink.

He thought of Rodrigo and his insides tightened uncomfortably. 'Before last week, I had not seen him in a long time.'

'He was exiled?' she murmured, and he was surprised. The history was well-known—though legitimacy had been given to Mauricio's actions, few understood that it was sheer self-interest that had governed his choices.

'Shortly after my parents died, yes.'

Her expression softened. 'Were you close?'

Memories blurred at the edges of his mind. Rodrigo catching him in his arms and tossing him into the air, his eyes crinkling with laughter, the way he played piano and sang along and played cards until far too late. The sense of safety and security he had, in those days, taken for granted—and never known again since. 'At one time, yes.' His voice was gruff. He cleared his throat. 'It was a long time ago.'

'Does that matter?'

His eyes met hers, burned through them. 'No.'

'How come you didn't see him, after he was exiled?'

'Until I was eighteen, I had very little autonomy. And after that, I didn't have the resources required to find him.'

'He disappeared?'

'He took the exile hard, apparently. I have learned a lot since my coronation. His life was far from a bed of roses.'

'In what way?' she asked, coming around from the

kitchen and standing close to him. So close he caught a hint of her perfume again, and this time when his gut rolled, he understood the feeling. Desire. Physical need. While he was an expert at maintaining relationships that were emotionally contained, he was still a red-blooded man with physical needs, and he indulged those needs as and when required.

'When he was exiled, he was cut off from his assets as well. He had some cash, but it wasn't enough to start a new life. He scraped by, but it was difficult for him.'

'And then he got sick?'

'He had AIDS,' Octavio murmured. 'And didn't realise. Medication now is so effective, he could have been treated, he could have lived a long life, but he didn't know and he didn't get help. So by the time I became King and launched a search for him, the disease had progressed and nothing could be done.'

'I'm so sorry,' she whispered. 'I still don't understand why he was exiled?'

Octavio's lips curled into a derisive smirk. 'That would require an explanation into the darker side of human nature and I'm not sure either of us want to go there tonight.'

She tilted her head a little, as if digesting his words. 'You don't want to talk about it?'

'There's no point. It's ancient history—nothing can be done now to right that wrong.'

'But you do think his exile was wrong?'

'Oh, I know it was.'

'And you couldn't do anything?'

'My uncle—my other uncle—had all the power of a king until I ascended the throne. It was his will, his way.'

'But we're talking about his younger brother?'

'Yes.'

'I don't understand. Why would he want him sent away? They're siblings.'

'Do you have a brother or sister?'

She shook her head. 'I always wished for one, but I was an only child.'

His expression shifted. 'As am I.'

'No spare to your heir?'

'No.' He didn't elaborate; it wasn't necessary. There was no need to go into the fact his parents tried for years after his birth, without success, to conceive another baby. Even as a young boy, he'd come to understand the vulnerability of his position. He'd always known that he would have to marry and have children—a reality he grappled with even now, because he would have preferred a solitary existence. An arranged marriage, though, offered some reassurance.

'Did you want a brother or sister?'

He'd never been asked that before. Then again, this was probably the most real conversation he'd had in a long time with anyone other than his cousin Xiomara.

'Not as a boy, but once my parents died, I wished for someone who understood what I was going through.'

'What about your other uncle?'

He bristled visibly. 'No.'

'Why not?'

'We weren't close.'

'Weren't? Aren't?'

'Both.'

'Because of the darker side of human nature?' she prompted.

His eyes scanned her face, studying her. She was different. Unusual. Though she'd insisted on using his title initially, she didn't seem at all nervous around him. She wasn't speaking to him with the exaggerated deference he was accustomed to, and he liked that.

'Yes.'

She expelled a small sigh. 'Would you like me to go?'

He frowned. 'Why do you say that?'

'You've clammed up.'

'I didn't mean to.'

'It's okay if you don't want to talk. I mean, if you'd rather be alone.'

He would always rather be alone. Except now, when his heart was splintering from the loss of his uncle and he wanted the distraction of *this*. A beautiful, warm, vibrant woman, keeping his mind occupied.

'I don't want to be alone.'

Her lips parted.

'I just don't want to talk about my family.'

Her smile was wry. 'I understand the feeling.'

He didn't push her. 'Have you worked here long?'

She shook her head. 'Just a couple of weeks. So you could say we both changed jobs around the same time,' she quipped.

He was surprised to feel a smile flash across his face.

'What did you do before this?'

She swallowed, and something crossed her features that made him wonder about more than just her vocation. He wondered about *her*. Her life, her history, what brought someone from a foreign country to Castilona, to work in a hospital as a cleaner.

'I was a receptionist at a school,' she murmured, but

her voice was strangled, her features tight. 'Back in New Zealand.'

'Touchy subject?'

She grimaced. 'Not really.'

But he saw through her. 'Phoebe?'

'Okay, a little.'

'What brings you to Castilona?'

She hesitated a moment. 'My birth father is from here.'

He waited for her to continue.

'I never knew him. He was on holiday in New Zealand when he met my mum. He never knew about me and she didn't know anything more than his name. She put him on my birth certificate but had no way of contacting him. All I know is that he may be here, somewhere.'

'And you want to find him?'

She nodded. 'I was raised to speak the language. My mum even tried to cook some of the more traditional meals. It was important to her that I have access to this side of my heritage even though I never met my father.'

'She must be happy you've travelled here then?'

'She passed away a few years ago.' Her voice was carefully controlled, but he could feel the emotion coming off her in waves, and his own grief was so close to the surface that he did something he wouldn't usually contemplate. He stepped closer and lifted a hand to her cheek. As soon as his fingertips connected with her skin, he realised he'd been wanting to do this from the moment he'd first laid eyes on her. She had reminded him of gossamer silk, and in the back of his mind he'd wondered if she'd feel so soft to touch. She did. Her skin was flawless and as he allowed his fingers to glide lower, she closed her eyes and let out a shuddering breath.

'Octavio,' she murmured, and now his name was soft with a plea, as though she were floating and asking him to catch her, to bring her back to Earth.

Only his body was driving him now, making him want to forget his grief, to live in the most vibrant of ways, to exist purely for feeling. His fingers shifted towards her mouth, so he could smooth his thumb across her lower lip. She let out a soft moan.

'This isn't a good idea,' she groaned, but her eyes met his and they were awash with the same sense of out-of-body need that was vibrating inside of him.

'Do you want me to stop?'

She lifted a hand to his chest, curling her fingers in his shirt as she stared up at him, totally bewildered. 'I didn't say that.'

His smile now was tight, his gut rolling with a visceral need. 'Do you want me to start?'

Her throat shifted as she swallowed. 'I—want—' Her teeth pressed into her lower lip and her eyes dropped to his mouth, lingering there so long he began to feel his skin tingle.

'Would you like me to kiss you, *querida*?'

Anguish flashed in her gaze, and surrender, too. She nodded slowly. 'Yeah, I think I'd like that.'

He didn't need to be asked twice, but caution was ingrained in Octavio. It came innately to him, and his position as heir presumptive and now King meant he had always focused on ensuring discretion with his private life. He wasn't an ordinary man, no matter what he wished.

'You understand I will leave for the palace tomorrow?'

She nodded softly.

'That my role will require me to disappear from your life?'

Her eyes narrowed. It was hardly the stuff of romance, but he knew from experience that it was better to be up-front about what he could offer.

'I know that.'

'It's only fair to be honest,' he explained.

'I agree.'

'I would appreciate it if you kept our interaction private.'

'But I have so many tabloids on my speed dial,' she responded archly. 'And I'm just itching to be known as a king's one-night stand.'

'Point taken. I'm sorry. I'm not myself tonight.'

Her features softened, sympathy gleaning in her eyes. 'That's understandable.' She lifted up onto the tips of her toes. 'Kiss me, Your Majesty.'

'Now who's being bossy?'

'Is that a complaint?'

His response was to crush her mouth with his own, his body rejoicing in the instant contact and connection and yes, vitality. He was alive. His blood rushed through his body, strength gathered in his muscles, and kissing her made every cell in his body reverberate with brilliant awareness. Best of all, death and loss and grief were nowhere now—there was only this.

CHAPTER TWO

DAWN STIRRED ACROSS the kingdom, like the breathing of fresh life into the night, a whisper and a kiss, light and gentle. Darkness turned to silver and then to mauve, before a hint of gold glimmered across the city, drawing Phoebe's eyes to the palace, which she glimpsed through the window.

What had seemed so natural and easy the night before now slammed into her with a growing sense of awe.

What had she done?

And *why*?

Phoebe had *never* had a one-night stand before in her life. In fact, she'd only been with one other man, whom she believed herself to be engaged to—little had she known, he was actually already married. But to Phoebe, it had been real, and she'd thought herself in love, and their intimacy had been a natural progression of that.

Last night with King Octavio had been something else entirely. Something wild and passionate, something quite feral, as if they were simply animals, unable to keep their hands off each other. Maybe it had started out as something else. Comfort? Sharing grief? An understanding of life's cruellest losses? But within minutes it had escalated. They'd torn clothes from one another, tangled arms and legs, lips meshed, bodies fused by a desperate, aching need that had refused to abate. The first time they were together had been wild and manic, but there'd been no answering calm afterwards. No sense of satiation. It had simply morphed into a different type of need, this time, a compulsion to explore slowly, to almost torment one another by holding back until they were once more at fever pitch. He'd kissed her all over, his mouth ravaging her breasts, her nipples, the sensitive skin just beneath her ear, her everywhere. She pressed the palm of her hand to her lips to contain a moan.

Dawn was breaking and she was *at work*. She needed to get out of the *clínica*, go home, freshen up and then get back to work, all without anyone knowing how she'd spent the small hours of the morning. Her heart was in her throat as she contemplated how exactly to handle the etiquette of the situation.

Last night, they'd agreed it was a one-night thing, and she'd been fine with that. She was still fine with it. Only, having known the mind-blowing pleasure that had been sex with Octavio, she was experiencing just a hint of remorse at the idea of leaving without one more kiss, one more everything...

But she had a shift starting in a few hours, which left just enough time to get home, shower, eat something and return. As quietly as she could, she crept from the bed, easing one leg out first and then the other, watching him the whole time, waiting to see if he would stir, half hoping he would even as she did her best to be quiet.

He didn't.

The combination of yesterday's grief and last night's activities must have worn him out, because she'd have put money on him ordinarily being an early riser. There was an intensity to him that made her think he was the kind of man who wouldn't want to waste a moment of the day.

Her clothes were in the lounge room, where they'd been flung the night before. She pulled them on quickly, tidied her hair, pinched her cheeks, then paused only to check her reflection in the mirror.

Phew.

She looked completely normal. There was no outward way to deduce how she'd spent last night.

Her handbag was still in the locker room, she realised with a groan, and she'd need it to get into her place. A slight complication, but she'd just have to try not to be seen by anyone who knew her well enough to be familiar with her shifts.

She crept out of the suite, shutting the door behind her as softly as possible, then moving quickly down the plush, carpeted corridor, head bent the whole way.

By some miracle, she managed it. Not only to retrieve her handbag, but also to slip out of the staff doors of the *clínica* without running into anyone she knew. She barely breathed until she'd boarded the bus that would take her within a few blocks of the apartment she was renting temporarily.

As she showered and dressed, her mind kept flashing back to last night. To the way he'd been with her. The way he'd kissed her and touched her as though she were the most perfect, rare, beautiful object in the world.

What a gift, to be able to make a woman feel like that. She'd never known anything like it.

She probably never would again.

She dismissed the thought. She wasn't thinking about

men or relationships right now. God knew, she'd been so badly burned by Christopher, she wasn't sure she'd ever trust anyone ever again. She couldn't so much as think of her ex without a horrible, all-consuming sense of shame. That she'd been 'the other woman', while he'd been married, got his wife pregnant, seen his first child born, and his second, all the while stringing Phoebe along, treating her like a first-rate idiot. And she had been an idiot, utterly and completely.

He'd been such an accomplished liar, though, it wasn't really that she was stupid. Just that she'd been alone and lonely and wanted to feel loved, and he'd offered her so much of that.

Memories of Christopher were just the antidote she needed to the swoony feelings Octavio had invoked. All men were bastards, she thought with satisfaction, as she dressed in her other uniform and prepared to return to work.

His first waking thought that day had been born of desire. He'd reached for Phoebe automatically, his arm stretching across the bed, his fingers seeking, wanting, needing, only to connect with the empty sheets. A cursory glance at the suite had shown him to be alone, and his instant reaction had been a visceral sense of disappointment before he'd told himself he should be relieved.

Despite his clarity the night before, there'd been a part of him that had worried she might want more than he was offering, that she might get the wrong idea. She was a cleaner in a hospital and he was royalty—was it possible she harboured some kind of romantic Cinderella notion?

Evidently not.

She'd disappeared, leaving no note, no number, nothing.

Until now. Standing in the foyer of the clinic, he listened as the director spoke gently.

'As there are no complicating factors, your uncle's body will be released as soon as you convey your wishes as to the funeral preparations. If you should wish for any further medical information, please—'

At that moment, there was a loud crash. One of his security agents had knocked an enormous vase of flowers to the tiled floor, leaving a cascade of water and stems in disarray.

'I'm so sorry, Your Majesty. Please excuse me a moment.'

Dr Garcia moved quickly, her heels clacking over the floor, and it was then that he saw her.

Phoebe James.

Phoebe James, who loved to be kissed just above her hip bone. Phoebe James, who had loved being on top last night, her body arching as she took him deep inside, her breasts so perfect and full, he hadn't been able to stop staring at them. Phoebe James, who'd run her hands all over him and moaned his name at the top of her lungs.

Phoebe James, with huge green eyes that were very determinedly *not* looking at him now, no matter how much he willed it.

Phoebe James, who was being instructed by her boss to clean up the mess his guard had just made.

Oh, for Christ's sake.

It was her job as a cleaner to clean things, but the sight of her scuttling across the tiles and scooping down, picking up the stems first and then moving on to the broken glass had him wanting to shout something. To force her to stop. The broken vase shouldn't be her responsibility. And he definitely shouldn't care this much, he admitted to himself. Not for some woman he'd just met and would never see again. But there was something about her that fired all his protective instincts to life.

So, when Lola, the director, returned to continue their conversation, he directly addressed the broken vase. 'That should not be your cleaner's responsibility. My guard knocked it—he will take care of it.'

'It's fine, Your Majesty. These things happen.'

Impotence grew inside of him. But how could he argue the point further without revealing something more? He had been worried about his own privacy the night before, but now he considered Phoebe's job. She had been such a stickler for convention initially; she hadn't even wanted to use his first name.

He listened as Lola continued to outline the protocols from here, but his eyes kept straying to Phoebe, and he was sure she knew he was watching, because her cheeks began to glow pink. At one point, a piece of glass cut her finger and he had to bite back a curse.

It was too much.

He strode across the tiles, uncaring for what Lola might think, and crouched beside Phoebe. Up close, memories of last night throbbed in his gut and spread through his whole body, so when he spoke his voice was raw with hunger. 'Let me help you.'

Startled, she looked at him, her lips parting. It was a mistake.

A huge mistake.

He couldn't help but stare at them, and the memories came thick and fast now. What would she say if he pulled her into his arms and kissed her until she was moaning against him, as she had the night before, begging for him to take her? He tamped down on that very real temptation. It would obviously be one of the stupidest things he could do, and Octavio was not stupid. Nor was he controlled by his libido. Generally.

'You're bleeding.'

'Go away.'

'You're hurt.'

'It's nothing, *please*.'

'Phoebe—'

'Don't,' she hissed, her eyes flashing past him, to the hospital director and whomever was watching. 'Please don't,' she whispered, plastering a bright smile on her face. 'This is my job.'

But he hated that.

His whole body was flush with emotions he couldn't process and didn't want to analyse. He continued to pick up pieces of glass.

'Your Majesty, you must stop,' she whispered. 'People will notice. People will talk.'

'Who gives a damn?'

'I do,' she promised. 'And you do, too. You've just forgotten it because of yesterday.'

Yesterday—his uncle's death. Not last night, with her. He shook his head once, to demur, but her features were so cold, her look so laced with warning. 'Please leave me alone,' she whispered.

He hated it.

He felt those words deep in the core of his being, and he couldn't say why but he knew that they mattered. He stood slowly, hands thrust into hips, looking down on her working, wishing it weren't this way. Wishing they were back in his bed, where they were thoroughly equals, wondering if he could move heaven and earth to make it so.

'Please go,' she whispered again, without looking up at him.

He turned on his heel and strode back to the clinic director, but Phoebe James was burned into his brain.

'The funeral was beautiful.' Octavio glanced at his cousin Xiomara without really seeing her. The funeral *had* been beautiful, Xiomara was right. Private, small and in accordance with royal traditions. Rodrigo had been brought home and laid to rest in the family crypt, reunited with his brother and parents.

'It was a good funeral, yes,' Octavio agreed.

Xiomara's smile was wistful. 'Thank you for letting my father attend.'

'I was surprised he wanted to.'

'I suppose time...' Her voice trailed off into nothing and she sighed. 'I can't defend it. You know that. But today was nice. You did well, Tavi.' She walked across and placed a kiss on Octavio's cheek. 'Do you need anything?'

Did he need anything? Hell, yes, he needed something. He needed the same thing he'd needed the night Rodrigo had died. The same thing he'd been craving every night since—or rather, someone. A craving he'd been fighting, because it was so out of his realm of experience, so overwhelming in a way he resented and instinctively shied away from.

He'd thought of calling Phoebe though, even when he knew it would be a mistake. But even if he'd wanted to, how could he? Apart from the fact he was now King, his every move tracked and speculated upon, he'd been manically busy dealing with the aftereffects of Rodrigo's death.

Funerals, though, were an end-point, a line in the sand, and now the background hum of noise that was his need for Phoebe had exploded into a full-blown absorption.

He wanted her in a way that was driving him to the point of distraction and then well beyond it. She had flooded him with something that night, something he'd become addicted to, even when he knew addiction was bad. Only, it would be problematic if he wasn't in control. If he let things really overtake him. But what if he could see her again whilst maintaining his usual vice-like grip on his emotions and strength?

Just once more. One more night.

Was there anything wrong with that? Octavio knew he wanted her more than he'd ever wanted another woman, but so long as he put a very clear end-point on this thing, what harm could come of it?

She had been discreet. There had been nothing in the papers about their tryst, no speculation online. He could trust her, just as he'd somehow known he could, even then. There'd been something about Phoebe's manner that had set her apart.

Or was it just that he'd wanted comfort and she'd been there, and for once in his life he hadn't worried about the consequences? It wasn't like Octavio to display such ambivalence. He trusted his instincts at all times—they'd served him well. And his instincts were pushing him, hard and fast, towards Phoebe and the comfort she could offer, and the pleasure they could share, just for one more night…

For a long time, Phoebe had held to a policy of ignoring calls from random numbers. They were always spammy sales calls, or lately would-be scammers, and she hated the interruptions. But she'd been making enquiries to find her father and was waiting on a return call from an investigator in the north of the country. So when her phone began to buzz and the screen showed *Number Withheld*, she swiped it to answer on the first ring. 'Phoebe James,' she said, stepping to the side of the footpath on which she'd been jogging, so she could concentrate.

Silence. A spam call, after all?

'Hello?'

More silence. She was about to hang up when a voice—deep, gruff, husky and immediately recognisable—came down the phone line. 'Phoebe, how are you?'

She almost dropped the phone in shock.

'Octavio!' His name was a breath from her lips. Out of nowhere, images of him, her, them flooded her mind. She gripped the railing that ran alongside the footpath. 'I—didn't expect to hear from you. How did you get my number?'

'Are you free right now?'

Her heart sped up. Her pulse throbbed. Her insides squirmed. Every part of her began to tremble and shake. She shook her head, even when she knew she would go to him, go wherever he asked her.

'Phoebe?'

'I can be,' she admitted. As if she had anything else

to do! She knew no one in the country, apart from a few acquaintances at work.

'I'm going to give you an address. Take a cab there, and then my driver will bring you the rest of the way.'

It took ten minutes to drive across town in the taxi she hailed, and by the time she arrived, a sleek black sedan with darkly tinted windows was waiting, a man in a suit standing near the rear door. She waited until the taxi driver had left before moving towards the car and taking a seat, and she fidgeted her fingers the whole way. The car drove through the winding streets that were so Castilonian she couldn't help but sigh at their obvious beauty. Old terracotta houses with wrought iron balconies, roof tiles and thick, green bushes which, in the light of day, would show shocks of colour. Red, purple, white geraniums and lavender, fragrant and stunning. The Mediterranean country was charmingly old-fashioned, and she felt a connection to it deep in her bones.

After around ten minutes, the car paused outside an old-fashioned-looking townhouse that had been adapted at some point to include an under-cover garage. The door lifted and the car drove into it. Phoebe's heart sped up as she briefly contemplated the potential risks of her decision to come here. She'd been so overwhelmed to hear his voice, so overwhelmed by a rush of need, but also concern, because the whole country had been talking about the funeral for his uncle and how that must be affecting the King. In the back of her mind, she'd worried for him all day, because she'd seen firsthand how Rodrigo's death had upset Octavio.

But here he was, standing in the garage, dressed in

suit trousers and a white shirt with the sleeves pushed up to his elbows. She stared at him from behind the tinted car window, greedily soaking up the image of him, only belatedly realising that she was wearing exercise gear and no make-up and wishing she'd somehow managed to squeeze in a quick trip back to her apartment to freshen up a little.

The door was opened by the driver, and then Octavio stepped forward, not smiling, his features set in a mask of intensity that took her breath away.

He held out a hand to help her from the car. As she put hers in his, she was conscious of her unpainted nails, cut short so they were easy to maintain, but then a spark travelled as if by magic from his fingers to hers, and all the way up her arm towards the very centre of her torso. She throttled a small gasp, low in her throat.

'I'm glad you came.'

She stood, so close to him she could feel his warmth. Her body tingled. 'How are you?'

He nodded once—what did that mean?—then put his hand on her lower back to guide her out of the garage, through a doorway and into a small entrance foyer that led to a set of polished timber stairs.

She walked ahead of him, up the stairs and into a stunning open plan living area with a whole wall of glass that overlooked a garden. Though it was night, the garden itself had beautiful lighting, showing the advanced trees and a water feature right in the middle.

'What is this place?'

'I lived here, before I became King. In many ways, I consider it to be my real home.'

She looked around with renewed interest. It was modern and sleek, a space that oozed elegance but not much warmth. She ran a hand over an end table, then turned her attention to Octavio. 'How did you get my number?' She'd asked him that on the phone, but he hadn't answered, and she wanted to know.

'It wasn't difficult.'

'I've only been in the country a short while, and I don't really know anyone...'

'But your employer has your details on file.'

She gasped. 'Tell me you didn't ask the *clínica* for my number?' Her heart sped up. She couldn't believe she'd got away unscathed after that night. She'd been waiting for the axe to drop, for someone to reveal that they'd seen her, but so far, nothing.

'No, *querida*. When my uncle was admitted and I announced that I would be spending time at the hospital, my head of security was given details of all employees so he could vet them.' Her jaw dropped. 'It was a necessary precaution.'

'Wow.' She pressed her fingertips to her temple. 'Okay, next question. Why did you call?'

His eyes traced her face for so long that she could *feel* heat on her skin, as if he was touching her. 'I needed to see you.'

Her stomach dropped to her toes. 'Did you?'

He nodded slowly, frowning a little, as if not sure what to say next. 'I needed you.'

Because of the funeral. Because he was grieving again, and she'd been such a successful answer to that last time. But did she care why he needed her? Hadn't she been craving him, too? That night hadn't been enough—

she wanted more. Just one more night? Would that cure her of this obsession?

'Phoebe, nothing's changed. Who I am, what I can offer...but I'm asking you to spend tonight with me.'

He was asking her. And he was being honest with her. Christopher had used her, he'd manipulated her, he'd broken her trust again and again. He'd made a fool of her, because he'd always been lying. The whole time they were together had been a falsehood. Octavio was being honest with her, and he was asking her what she wanted. This was her choice; she could do what she wanted, on her terms.

And she knew what she wanted.

'Yes,' she said, simply, walking towards him with a sense of purpose she had no interest in doubting. 'I'll spend tonight with you.'

CHAPTER THREE

THE NEXT MORNING he reached for her, just as he had the other morning, only this time, his fingertips glanced across soft, smooth flesh, her body warm and close. He didn't know what time it was. Light was filtering through the windows of his bedroom, but it was still a pale, golden light, promising the freshness of a just burgeoning day.

She shifted in her sleep, rolling to face him, her eyes shut, her lashes long against her creamy skin. Her lips curved into a smile. He closed the distance between them, kissing her slowly, softly, savouring this moment of waking her, his naked body pressed to hers, so she responded immediately. Her arm snaked around his middle, her mouth moved beneath his, and deep in her throat she moaned, a husky sound filled with need.

He moved his body over hers, delighting in the feel of her nakedness beneath him, of her responsiveness to his touch, delighting in his power over her. As he moved his hands, he was invoking a powerful, age-old spell, stirring her body to fever pitch with every brush of his fingers, every movement of his mouth. She was soft and supple, her skin lifting in goose bumps with his touch, her body reacting with warmth and need. His kisses dragged across her flesh, padding the goose bumps with his lips, his tongue, tracing her lines. He worshipped her sex with his mouth, his strong hands on her thighs, holding her apart for him, so he had total access to her most private, sensitive core.

She bucked against his mouth, her body beaded in fine perspiration, her moans louder and faster now, so he grinned as he pulled away from her purely to grab a condom and then returned, his own need an insatiable beast controlling him completely.

He nudged her legs apart and thrust into her hard, deep, her muscles squeezing him tight, her whole body reacting to his presence, her cries filling the room with that particular note of fervent need. His own cries were low but no less infused with desperation; he was buried inside of her, but it wasn't enough. He moved faster, kissed her harder, his tongue an unconscious echo of his movements, his hair-roughened chest brushing against her hardened nipples. Her hands ran down his back, cupped his buttocks, held him where she needed him, and then she was screaming his name as her whole body began to tremble and the muscles that were surrounding him began to tighten almost unbearably, making restraint impossible. He came almost as she did, losing himself to this overwhelming sensation of pleasure, his body throbbing with satiation, his release intense.

He collapsed on top of her, burying his face in the crook of her neck, feeling every deep, rasping breath she took, hearing it inside his own body. This had started as a distraction, as a need to forget, but it was now just simply *need.* He contemplated rolling away from Phoebe and then ending this. He thought about not seeing her again, and he knew he wouldn't do it. He didn't want to.

There was something about her that made his body sing, and he wasn't ready to give it up yet. Even when it was the right thing to do. While his betrothal had never been formalised, it was very much expected by both royal households. His parents' wishes, and her parents' wishes, were in alignment, and Octavio had always known he would honour his parents' choice for him.

But his marriage was still some time off. It would take at least a year to finalise arrangements and prepare the ceremony. Until then, he was a free agent. Free to do what he wanted, but not if that proved harmful to Phoebe.

He pushed up onto his elbow so he could see her more clearly. Her beautiful face was flushed pink, her eyes wide as she stared at him.

'Good morning,' she murmured, running her fingers through her hair.

He shifted his hips a little, revelling in the way she bit into her lip. Sensations were still flooding his body, and he was sure she was also feeling the aftereffects of their coming together.

He wanted more of her; but how much more? And for how long? It wasn't fair to use Phoebe to fill a gap in his life while it suited him, then discard her when he was ready to marry. Besides, he had no idea what she wanted.

Everything between them was incredibly simple and organic—it just felt easy. At the same time, it was also impossibly hard. He had been born to serve his country; that was his duty. It was something he'd always known, but after the death of his parents it had crystallised in his mind as the primary purpose in his life. He had focused on that every single day after their deaths, when his uncle had made his life a misery, and his nannies had delighted in punishing him and isolating him, he'd thought of his country and the kind of King he would be, how he could make his parents proud. It was the sole focus of his life.

He wasn't interested in relationships—not relationships that might take that focus and split it. Particularly not now he was finally in the box seat and had been crowned King. He needed to work hard to undo the damage Mauricio had wrought, and then he needed to marry the Princess his parents had chosen and create enough heirs that the line of succession would be safe for ever. These were his priorities. Not losing time and energy to a woman. Not even a woman as tempting as Phoebe. In fact, she was so tempting that she reminded him how important it was to walk away from her—to remind them both that this was meaningless and unimportant, because nothing mattered to him like his role as King did.

A heaviness sat in his chest as he mentally closed the door on temptation. He wanted Phoebe, but he couldn't have her, and he'd known that right from the start of this thing.

'I'll have my driver take you home.'

Even to his own ears, his voice was cold; no wonder she flinched a little. The light that had seemed to glitter in her eyes was instantly extinguished. Her lips parted on a soft sound of breath escaping. He could see her physically wrangling with his meaning, trying to interpret it differently, and watching the shift in her emotions was something he didn't enjoy. He wanted to apologise. To explain. To help her understand that she was wonderful but he was limited, so limited, in what he could offer and even what he could want. But for some reason, he couldn't properly grasp how to vocalise any of those feelings. He couldn't even properly shape the explanations in his own mind, so how could he offer them to her?

With growing frustration and a sense that he'd bitten off more than he could chew, Octavio pulled away from her, the separation almost a physical pain. He turned his back, strode across the room, stepping into his bathroom and closing the door. Only then did he expel the breath he'd been holding.

He made it five weeks. Five weeks without weakening and calling Phoebe. Five weeks without getting his driver to take him to her place, so Octavio could knock on the door and apologise for the ice-cold way he'd ended things that morning. Five weeks in which sleep had been made almost impossible because of the nature of his dreams and the strength of his wants. Five weeks in which he'd pushed himself to work long days in the hope he would be tired enough to get her from his mind and actually find some kind of relief.

For things to go back to normal.

But nothing was normal. In the space of a couple of months, he'd turned twenty-eight, ascended the throne, witnessed his beloved uncle's death and got to grips with the parlous state his other uncle had left the country in. And met Phoebe.

Phoebe, who was beautiful and fascinating but in no way suitable to be anything more than a secret fling. A cleaner from New Zealand was not exactly the kind of woman his parliament and advisors would expect him to date, let alone do anything more serious with.

In any event, a relationship with Phoebe was a moot point. His betrothal loomed, which meant he shouldn't have been thinking about Phoebe at all.

Never mind that he had known for a long time he wasn't interested in a relationship that had the ability to monopolise his mind and worse, his heart. Not that his heart was involved in his calculations. He'd slept with Phoebe, that was all. He hardly knew her beyond that. It didn't matter that there was something about her that was different from the women he'd been with in the past; she was unsuitable for any part in his life. And even if she had been serious, when he was with her a part of him, a deep, important part, had turned into a bright red flag, warning him to be careful.

So couldn't he see her *and* still be careful? Couldn't he create parameters that would keep them *both* safe from the sort of vulnerabilities he sought to avoid?

The thought kept rolling around and around in his mind though, and eventually, he found it impossible to ignore.

Maybe there was one way in which he could see Phoebe, in some capacity, if she were willing. Just maybe he could make something work with her, just for a while. Just maybe he could have his cake and eat it, too…

Phoebe could not have been more shocked if a Martian had been on the other side of the door. 'What are you doing here?'

'His Majesty asked me to speak to you.'

She stared at Octavio's driver, anger blooming as

though it hadn't been five long weeks since he'd all but dismissed her. He hadn't gone so far as to thank her for services rendered, but he might as well have. That was exactly how he'd made her feel. Cheap, and used.

'Yeah, well, I have no interest in anything His Bloody Majesty might have to say.' She went to slam the door in the driver's face but his foot caught the door before it latched.

'I'm afraid I can't take no for an answer.'

'That's your problem,' she snapped. 'You can take it or leave it, but my answer is still no.'

This time, when she slammed the door, he didn't stop it.

She should have known better than to believe that would be the end of it. Only two minutes later, with hands still trembling from outrage, in the midst of making a mug of peppermint tea, the doorbell rang once more. *Damned persistent driver*, she thought with chagrin, making her way into the small foyer and wrenching it inwards.

Only to find Octavio staring back at her, all unmistakable royal importance and unfairly perfect good looks.

'What are you doing here?'

'You left me no choice.'

'We always have a choice,' she replied, gripping the door.

'Mind if I come in?'

She cast a glance over her shoulder, aware that her place was as tidy as usual, but still hating the thought of Octavio seeing where she was living. It was only temporary, a place to stay whilst she searched for her father, but it was still a reflection of her. It was intimate. Exposing.

Only in that brief moment, rather than waiting for an answer, he swept past her, brushing his body to hers by virtue of the cramped entrance area, so her pulse went haywire.

She stood there, staring at him, door still open, so Octavio made a noise of impatience, reached over and unpeeled her fingers. Just his touch sent a thousand little fireworks into her veins. She jumped back from him, holding on to her anger as though it were an anchor she desperately needed.

'What do you want?' Before he could answer, she clicked her fingers in the air, and when she spoke her voice was heavy with sarcasm. 'Oh, let me guess. A quick roll in the hay? What's gone wrong in your life today that you need me to fix, Your Majesty? A problem with the budget? A servant? Did you come here to sleep with me so you could forget something else?'

His features were locked in a mask of steel, giving nothing away, and she was glad. If he'd looked even slightly chastened or apologetic, she might have softened her anger a little. Instead, he stared back at her with a look of cynicism and *nothing*.

Nothing.

He'd come here and he was looking at her as though it was the last place he wanted to be.

Damn him.

'What do you want?' she demanded, her tone as withering as she could make it. In the back of her mind, she wondered if he'd ever been spoken to like that. She couldn't help it though. His quick change of heart and immediate dismissal of her once she had performed her purpose had resonated so perfectly with the feelings she'd suffered on that awful day when the penny had finally dropped and she'd realised how utterly and completely Christopher had been using her. Octavio hadn't done anything nearly as bad as Christopher, but Phoebe had a big, open wound that Octavio had unknowingly and deeply plunged a knife into.

'Is there some place we can talk?'

She gestured to the small foyer as if to say *here*, only it was *small* and he was *big* and there was a sudden dearth of space that made it hard for Phoebe to think. With an angry expulsion of breath, she whirled away from him and practically stomped into the living room.

Small, but neat as a pin, it was light-filled and perfectly adequate for the six months or so Phoebe intended to stay in Castilona. After that, she expected her savings to have run out, and if she hadn't managed to find her father in that time, she'd go home and work out how to get on with her life. At least she would have succeeded in putting some space and distance between herself and the disastrous breakup with Christopher.

'Okay, talk,' she said, then added with faux deference, 'Your Majesty.'

She was used to seeing Octavio smile, but this time, when his lips shifted into a general approximation of that expression, there was no humour in his face. Rather, it was a look of cynicism, or even mockery.

'You're angry with me.'

She crossed her arms. 'Do you blame me?'

'Why are you angry?' he prompted.

She stared at him as if he'd just asked what feet were used for. 'I would imagine it's pretty obvious.'

'Humour me.'

'Why?'

'Because I'd like to understand what I'm dealing with before I start.'

'Start what?'

'What I came here for.'

'Are you being deliberately cryptic?'

'I asked you first.'

'What are you, eight?'

He didn't answer. Those dark, mesmerising eyes of his just bore into her, and as the seconds ticked by, the force of his look and the caustic silence surrounding them eroded her strength. She lifted one shoulder in a gesture of conversational surrender. 'You were rude.'

One thick, dark brow arched upwards.

'I knew what you wanted from me, and why, but I still never expected you to make me feel so disposable. I thought you were...*nice*.' It was a very insipid way to explain what she'd thought of him. She'd *liked* him. She'd thought he was *nice*, yes, but also kind and funny and decent. In short, she'd been fooled, just like with Christopher. Would she never learn?

'You are not disposable,' he said, but the words were tinged with something like anger. 'If you were, I would not be here now.'

'Why are you here?'

'To explain.'

'There's no point. It's over. Ancient history. I don't even think about it any more.'

Another quirk of his brow and this time, his quick half-smile was definitely, unmistakably mocking. 'Don't you?'

'No.' She doubled down on the slight exaggeration.

She thought about it, him, what they'd done from time to time. As in, at least several times a day. Most days, even more often than that. 'It's old news.'

'Prove it,' he growled, taking a step towards her.

Her throat felt thick suddenly, her bones liquid. 'How?'

He pressed a finger to her chin. 'Show me I'm old news. Don't react when I kiss you, Phoebe, and I'll believe you.'

She opened her mouth to protest but he took the opportunity to drop his mouth to hers and kiss her. Oh, she could have pulled away, kneed him in the groin, shoved at his chest, elbowed him in the ribs. When she looked back, she realised he'd deliberately hesitated a few seconds—between laying down the gauntlet and making good his threat, he'd given her time to respond, to push him away. But she hadn't.

Because even when she knew her body would show her to be a liar, she didn't—couldn't—care. She just wanted him to kiss her.

She did her best not to respond as his mouth separated hers and his tongue invaded every single one of her senses. She tried to think cold, practical thoughts as his fingers tangled in the hair at the back of her head. She willed her body to stay completely still, as if frozen, as he pushed himself forward, his large frame easily engulfing her smaller one. And for several long seconds, she managed. She stayed almost limp against him, refused to kiss him back, refused to show that her heart was beginning to pound dangerously fast and her pulse was thready.

But then his knee caught a little between her legs, and

the moan that escaped her was impossible to resist. It was like opening the floodgates. All the desire she'd felt and had no place for in the last five weeks suddenly went from gas to flame, and her whole body was alight with passionate wants. They stirred in her belly and spread throughout, so not only was she kissing him back, her hands were roaming his body, separating his shirt from his trousers and lifting it so she could touch the warm flesh of his bare back.

'I hate you.' She groaned against him, though she wasn't sure if that was true. She hated Christopher, and how he'd made her feel, and she hated that Octavio had unwittingly found that old emotional injury and reinflamed it, proving that she wasn't anywhere near healed yet. Maybe she never would be.

'But you want me,' he said, moving his kiss to her throat, flicking the pulse point there with his tongue, which he clearly knew drove her wild. 'And that's the most important thing.'

'Is it?' She tilted her head back to give him better access.

'Oh, absolutely, *querida*. It's all that matters.' And then he was cupping her breasts and the last vestiges of thought dispersed so she was just a quivering mass, his to do with what he would. And he understood that moment of surrender. It was as though she were a book and he could read her just perfectly. He pushed her shirt over her head, growling when he realised she wore no bra, but not hesitating before taking one of her nipples into his mouth and rolling it mercilessly, until she was incandescent. He moved a hand down her belly, finding the fastening to her jeans and pushing it open so that he could slide his hand into her underpants and brush her sex. She whimpered; he moved his mouth to absorb the sound, kissing her while his other hand turned its attention to her breast, squeezing the nipple that was already oversensitive.

'Please,' she groaned. 'God, please.'

His response was a gruff sound of surrender and then he was stripping them both of their clothes with an efficiency Phoebe couldn't have managed, given how badly her hands were shaking. Naked, he lifted her easily, wrapping her legs around his waist, so his arousal was nestled between the cheeks of her bottom. She rolled her hips, silently inviting, needing, desperately hungry for him. He made a deep sound of understanding and strode through the apartment, his lips seeking hers as he walked.

'Where?' he grunted.

She pointed to her bedroom door. Octavio shouldered it open and dropped her to the bed, his eyes firing to hers as he ripped open a condom she hadn't even realised he'd brought with them. Then again, in his position, he couldn't exactly take chances, and God knew she didn't want to run that risk either.

He unfurled it over his length and then he was moving over her, pushing inside of her, and she cried out at the sheer relief her body felt to have him filling her once more. The world seemed to stop spinning and every noise silenced, so there was only the solid racing of their hearts.

'Octavio...' She said his name long and slow, like a prayer that had been answered, and then she said noth-

ing else, because he moved in such a way that made
her body come alive and rendered her mouth mute—
save for the little moans of ecstasy that escaped without her knowledge.

CHAPTER FOUR

WHEN THE DUST settled and her breathing returned to normal—though pleasure was still a fog wrapping around her body—sanity began to return, and Phoebe was nervous.

Nervous because she'd let this happen again, even after the way he'd been, last time. Nervous because he might treat her like that again, and if he did, what did that mean for her decision-making?

She'd come here to find her father, but also to grieve and move forward from the Christopher debacle. She needed to heal, to find peace and to reassure herself that she was capable of exercising some solid judgement with men. But wasn't this falling into the same trap? Being so blinded by desire that she couldn't think straight?

Well, if he thought he could just come to her apartment for sex and then leave again, he had another think coming. She wasn't going to lie there, waiting for him to make her feel worthless. If anyone was going to get up and leave, it would be her.

Despite the fact that her bones were heavy and her muscles like liquid, thanks to the pleasure he'd lavished on her, and despite the fact she liked how it felt to lie right there, cradled to his side, she quickly jerked away, turning her back on him before standing and going to her chest of drawers. She pulled out a summery dress and yanked it over her head, not worrying about underwear, before turning to face him. 'Do you need anything else?' She crossed her arms over her chest, ignoring the look of wry amusement on his face.

How dare he?

'We still have a conversation to get through.'

Pink bloomed in her cheeks. 'I can't see that we have anything to talk about.'

'Really? Would you like another demonstration?'

She bit down into her lower lip and refrained—just—from telling him that maybe she would. 'That doesn't mean anything.'

He sat up a little straighter, the sheet draped over his lap. Her sheet. Would she ever wash it again? She banished the errant thought, narrowing her gaze.

'Doesn't it?'

'No.'

'I'm glad to hear you say that.' He nodded slowly, as if that had been exactly what he wanted to hear. 'How would you feel about coming to a sort of arrangement?'

Lights danced on the edge of her field of vision. 'What do you mean, an arrangement?'

'Obviously, this works.' He ran his hand over the bed beside him. 'I like being with you, Phoebe. In fact, in all sincerity, I have been able to think of very little but you for the last five weeks.' She smothered a small gasp—but barely. 'Which, as I'm sure you can imagine, is not particularly convenient, given my responsibilities.'

She ignored the flush of pleasure his confession wrought. But it meant a lot to know that he'd been as afflicted by desires and memories as she had been. Careful to keep her expression neutral, she fidgeted one hand behind her back. 'So? Where are you going with this?'

'A long time ago, my parents entered into a sort of contract with King Stanos and Queen Margerite. It's more an agreement of intent, rather than legally binding. However, my plan has always been to honour it.'

'What kind of contract?' She wasn't following—perhaps because the sheer force of her pleasure not two minutes ago had robbed her brain of most of its blood.

'A marriage contract. They have a daughter—Sasha. She's three years younger than I am. It was always their intention that we would marry.'

Phoebe stood very, very still but inside, her heart was turning to ice faster than she could handle. He kept talking, evidently oblivious to the pain he was inflicting.

'They felt—as I feel now—that a royal marriage would be best. To secure our family's position on the throne.'

Octavio wasn't Christopher, but echoes of the moment she'd met Christopher's wife and had needed to act as though everything was perfectly fine made her whole world spin wildly out of control. The hand that had been fidgeting behind her back flattened so she could press it to the wall for much-needed support.

'Why are you telling me this?'

'Because if you're going to agree to my proposal, I need to be perfectly clear about the boundaries of what I'm offering.'

She blinked quickly. 'What proposal?'

But there was a sinking feeling in her stomach that showed she already understood. Still, she waited, with breath held, needing to hear him say the words and confirm her worst fears.

'I want you to be my lover, *querida*. I want to see you for as long as we feel like this, for as long as it works, and for as long as I am able.'

She flinched. 'You mean until you're married?'

'Until the engagement is formalised,' he corrected. 'Anything beyond that would not be right.'

She made a scoffing sound, half laughter, half deranged disbelief. 'No, of course. Whereas this is all perfectly above board.'

He studied her, as if trying to read her every thought. She hated that. She hated him. She hated what he was making her feel—worthless and cheap, all over again. She ground her teeth, glaring back. 'And what would be in it for me?' she demanded. 'You get sex whenever you want it. What do I get?'

'The same thing. No one could know about it—this would be between you and me.'

'Why?'

'It's for the best.'

'Because I'm a cleaner?'

'You would be hounded by the press, and to what end? This could only last another six months or so, at the most.'

'So you're telling me the fact I work as a cleaner at a hospital has no bearing on how you'd feel being seen with me?'

'I don't care what you do for a living, Phoebe.'

'Sure you don't,' she scoffed.

'But other people would,' he conceded after a beat. 'That is not why I would need this kept secret. I don't care

what people say, but my uncle—who until recently was
on the throne—has worked hard to undermine me, even
before I was crowned. I would prefer to avoid scandal.'

'And I'm a scandal.'

'Potentially. So we could go between the house of
mine we used the other night and your apartment. I also
have homes around the world—we could travel together,
when our schedules allowed.'

Just like a real high-class mistress, she thought with
a wave of nausea.

Outwardly, she made another scoffing noise. 'You've
really thought all this through, haven't you?'

'I've had five long weeks to come up with a plan.'

'And this was the best you could do?'

'Well, what do you suggest?' he demanded. 'What
other option is there?'

'That we go back to Plan A and never see one another again.' Her voice was shrill now, control on her
emotions almost non-existent. She needed him to leave
before she reached for the crystal vase beneath the window and hurled it at him.

'I do not believe that's viable.'

'Nor is this.'

'Why not?'

'Because I won't be treated like some kind of…of…
whore!' she spat, slicing her hand through the air. 'I won't
become your mistress. No way.'

'You would be my lover,' he corrected gently, standing now, uncaring for his magnificent nudity as he strode
towards her. 'Here, and at my apartment, we would be
equals. Two people who can spend time together, make
love whenever they want, until this madness passes.'

She flinched. 'And then you ride off into the sunset and marry Princess Whatever-Her-Name-Is?'

'Sasha,' he supplied gently. 'And yes.'

'And what about me, Octavio?'

'You move on with your life, too. This would be our arrangement, Phoebe. *Our* arrangement. I am not dictating terms to you, I am asking you to be a party to a deal that enables us to keep seeing one another.'

It was all so reasonable and sensible, but Phoebe didn't feel either of those things. She felt sickened by his suggestion and she felt mad. Mad up to the eyeballs! She wanted to scream at the insult he was wrapping around her, and somehow expecting her to be almost relieved about. 'It's not enough,' she spat. 'I don't want what you're offering.'

'I can't offer more.'

'Then I don't want you.'

'But you do, and we both know it,' he said, with a hint of regret, because they were both trapped, in a sense, by this desire. 'The question is, do you want me enough to accept this deal?' He gently caught her chin with his finger and angled her face up to his. 'I really hope the answer is yes.'

Tears threatened to form on her lashes. She blinked quickly, squaring her shoulders. 'It's not. Now please, get the hell out of my apartment and don't ever contact me again.' And with her last thread of strength, she pulled away from him and stalked out of her bedroom.

He knew he should have left straight away, but he was reeling. He had come here with no expectation that she would refuse him. In the back of his mind, he'd seen the

arrangement as a *fait accompli*. He'd been almost unfor-
givably rude the last time they'd seen one another, but
their chemistry was such, he'd fully expected it to over-
come any obstacle. More than that, the parameters he'd
put in place surely made the whole concept of this safe
and easy and even fun. At least, that's how he viewed it.
The perfect non-relationship relationship.

Instead, every word he'd said after they'd finished
making love had seemed to rile her more and more. But
he hadn't been wrong about her feelings for him—on a
physical level, she was as invested in this as he was. So
why was she fighting him?

'Listen, Phoebe.' He followed after her, hands raised
in a placating gesture. 'This doesn't have to be a big
deal. Let's leave it a week and then touch base. If you're
available, you can come to my place for dinner. We can
talk more.' Perfect. Casual. Easy. As though he didn't
care one way or another—he just wished that were true.

The jut of her chin was laced with defiance; she might
as well have sky-written *No way*.

'Just think about it,' he said, because he wasn't ready
for this conversation to be over, and he didn't think she
was either. Once her initial reaction faded, she'd calm
down, think this through and realise that he was offering
them a way to be together that was easy, uncomplicated
and had the potential to be endlessly satisfying—for as
long as possible.

Phoebe waited until he'd left before giving into the nausea that had gripped her from the moment he'd made his
hurtful proposition. He couldn't have known how badly
he was wounding her, but Phoebe had—unwittingly—

been a mistress before. For years she'd been falling in love with someone else's husband, and she wasn't about to make the same mistake twice. Okay, he wasn't offering love. It was even worse. He just wanted to sleep with her, all the while formalising his engagement to some far-away princess. Not bloody likely!

Indignation flared in her belly, but so too did a wave of nausea she'd struggled to contain while they were arguing. Now he was gone, she bolted for the bathroom and kneeled over the toilet, shuddering with each violent expulsion, vomiting until her brow was beaded with sweat and her face flushed pink.

If only it were so easy to push Octavio from her mind…

Six weeks had passed since that afternoon at Phoebe's, and over the course of that time, Octavio had come to accept that she'd been serious in her refusal. She might have wanted him with the same intensity as he did her, but she was clearly determined not to fall in with his convenient arrangement.

And maybe that was for the best. Because he'd presumed they were in the same place, and wanted the same things—no strings—but her reaction had indicated otherwise, and emotional complications were the last thing Octavio wanted. So it was fine that she'd turned him down.

Just fine.

Except when it wasn't, which was most nights. And often in the days, when his mind wandered and he remembered the smoothness of her skin or the softness of her lips or how tightly her muscles squeezed his length, how good she made him feel.

His pride had been wounded, he accepted. That was why he was so focused on this. It wasn't really about Phoebe, or his need for her, so much as the fact she'd turned him down—and so easily. As though he meant nothing.

So maybe it wasn't just his pride, but rather an old, familiar, awful sense of cold-hearted rejection. A feeling he'd had so often in his childhood he thought he'd inured himself to its effects, but if that were true, then being turned down by Phoebe wouldn't have bothered him as much as it did. He knew the best defence to that feeling was to wall it up, ignore it. And certainly never show anyone how you were feeling.

So when he walked into the Clínica San Carlos for an appointment with director Lola Garcia, he was frustrated to realise his eyes were constantly sweeping the corridors as if seeking her out. Did she even still work here? And what kind of a weak-minded idiot did it make him that he still couldn't get her out of his head?

If only she'd agreed to his suggestion, he'd have probably got her out of his system by now. Or at least be partway there.

But Phoebe James was burned into his blood, and he halfway hated her for that, because it made a mockery of his determination to never need anyone. Even if that need was purely physical, it was still an exertion of power over him that he resented bitterly.

'Your Majesty.' Lola dipped her head in a gesture of deference. Beside her, the hospital's head of security kept a watchful eye on the entrance to Lola's office. His attention was superfluous. Octavio was accompanied by his usual security detail, and he knew the hospital had a state-of-the-art system in place. There was no threat to him here.

Then again, hadn't his parents thought the same thing? When was someone in his position ever truly safe?

'Dr Garcia,' he responded, itching to continue prowling the hallway until he saw Phoebe. Just a glimpse, to prove he was over his stupid infatuation. Octavio had worked hard to conquer his obsession with Phoebe, and he wanted proof that he'd been successful. He was not about to let one woman he happened to share insane chemistry with weaken his ability to rule. No, he was focused on the future now, and on the engagement that was becoming inevitable. 'Thank you for seeing me.'

'Of course, Your Majesty. Anytime.' She took a seat behind her desk. 'Is there something in particular I can help you with?'

'Actually, I'd like to help you.' He crossed one ankle over his knee and braced an elbow on his thigh, staring directly at her. 'I appreciate the care your staff took of my late uncle. His passing was a tragedy, but the loss was made a little less difficult by your hospital's professionalism and care.'

Lola looked genuinely moved.

'I would like to make a large donation to the hospital—a personal donation, you understand—and I would like the donation to be in his name. In fact, I would greatly appreciate the naming of a wing after him.'

Lola's jaw dropped and he knew why. Even hospitals as lavish as this struggled with funding. Providing top-notch healthcare was expensive and in order to attract the best staff in the business, you had to pay well and have exceptional facilities. All of which cost a bomb.

'I'm talking about a substantial sum, you understand.' He reached into his shirt pocket and retrieved the cheque he'd had drawn from his personal wealth, handing it over to the director.

'Your Majesty.' Lola's voice was barely a whisper. 'That's very generous of you.'

'You do good work here, Dr Garcia. It's my privilege to make this donation, in my uncle's name.'

'I don't know what to say.' Her fingers were shaking a little, but she didn't relinquish the cheque.

'There is nothing to say—please, keep me apprised of how you decide to honour Rodrigo.'

'Of course. Sir, would you like to have a tour of the hospital facilities? I know you have been here, but in circumstances that might have prevented you from seeing everything we do. Once you've witnessed the wards, you might have ideas on how you'd like to see the donation used.'

'You are best placed to know how to spend the money in a way that will benefit the hospital. But,' he said, pleased that his voice sounded completely normal, 'I would welcome a chance to look around.'

Lola stood and handed the cheque to her chief of security. 'Don't lose that.'

'No, ma'am.'

They stepped into the corridor, and Octavio's own security entourage followed behind. The tour lasted some thirty minutes and though he spotted several other cleaners wearing the same fitted navy blue uniform as Phoebe, they were not her.

Right at the end, as he was preparing to say farewell to Lola Garcia, he thought, for a moment, that he'd finally glimpsed her. The hair was the same, and the tone of skin, but this woman had a different figure. Larger breasts, perhaps even a slightly rounded stomach, indicating pregnancy.

And Phoebe wasn't pregnant. Or at least, she hadn't been, the last time he'd seen her.

Unless…

Even before the thought could fully form, she angled her body away from the wall, showing not just the fact that yes, her stomach was indeed rounded in that way of pregnancy, but also a face that was burned into his brain, eyes that were as familiar to him as his own. He stared across at her and noted the exact moment she glanced up and saw him. He recognised the colour being sucked from her face, the parting of her lips, the panic in her features. And he recognised, even before it happened, that her knees were about to buckle.

'She's fainting,' he said to no one in particular, breaking into a jog and reaching Phoebe just as her legs gave way and she began to fall to the ground. He caught her, but only just, enabling him to ease her slowly down and save her head from cracking against the marble tiles.

'Oh, my goodness.' Lola Garcia was right behind him. 'Enrique, get a nurse.'

'I'm okay.' Phoebe had momentarily fainted, but she'd also recovered quickly. Her skin was regaining a hint of colour and her eyes were focused on Octavio, as if trying to work out if he was really there or not.

'It's you.'

'I'm sorry, Your Majesty,' Lola murmured with concern. 'She's obviously still not with it.'

'She seems with it enough to me,' he responded, his brain not able to put two and two together and get four, even when the number was flashing in front of him in neon.

Phoebe was pregnant.

But not too far along. Her belly was only noticeably rounded because she was so naturally slim. And only because he knew her body inch by inch and would have noticed even the smallest of differences.

'I'm okay,' Phoebe repeated, pushing away a little now, trying to stand. He watched as she sat up first, then went to bend her knees, but it was evident that she was still too woozy. Besides, Lola wasn't having a bar of it.

'You'll have to be checked out and signed off by a doctor. It's a workplace health and safety issue, you see.'

'I only fainted. It's nothing,' Phoebe said, not daring to look at Octavio.

'Yes, well, we can't be too careful, particularly not in your condition.'

Phoebe's face scrunched up, and Octavio realised she'd been holding on to some kind of fool's hope that he hadn't realised she was pregnant.

'Director Garcia is right,' Octavio said, his voice so darkly menacing he didn't recognise it. 'A pregnant woman cannot be too careful.'

Phoebe's eyes jerked to his and he saw the panic in their depths and he was glad. Almost as glad as he was livid. Phoebe James had seriously crossed a line and he was going to make sure she knew it.

CHAPTER FIVE

PHOEBE WAS REELING. Her mind was spinning and it wouldn't stop. On top of the shock of seeing Octavio for the first time in six weeks, and knowing he had *seen her*, was the news the doctor had delivered after her fainting episode.

In an exercise in 'above and beyond' care, they'd done an ultrasound to check on her pregnancy. Phoebe hadn't had one yet, and she was close enough to twelve weeks for it to be time. She'd been grateful when they'd suggested it—one less thing for her to take care of.

But as the room filled with a cacophony of beats, and the doctor had turned to her, beaming, he'd said, 'Well, well, aren't you clever? It's twins!' Phoebe had almost fainted again.

Twins.

Twins.

She'd just been getting her head around the fact that she was going to be a single mother to *one* baby—a task she knew from experience to be one of the hardest in the world. But a single mother to *two* children? She felt hot and cold.

So when she emerged from the *clínica* a little while later and saw Octavio's driver waiting for her, she wanted to refuse to go anywhere with him. But even though she was in shock, she knew there was no chance Octavio would let this matter drop. In a total fog, she slid into the back seat of the car, her mind racing as the sleek limousine slipped through the streets of the city. She didn't notice the beauty of the place, the beaches she loved, the Mediterranean buildings all rendered in shades of orange and cream, the paved paths and laundry strung from window to window. She noticed nothing, *nada*.

Her whole body was in a state of suspended animation.

'There's paparazzi waiting,' the driver said with a tone of apology as the car slowed.

Phoebe looked around, belatedly realising they were not at the townhouse she'd expected to be taken to, but rather approaching Octavio's palace. Her breath hitched in her throat at the sight of this place, which was so utterly beautiful it almost hurt.

The ornate wrought iron gates with their gold spikes and large coat of arms swung inwards. On either side of their car, several guards stood in military uniform, their large guns displayed proudly at their front. Gravel crunched beneath the tyres as the car rolled forward, towards the front of the palace, where a large golden fountain was spurting water. There were several archways in the façade of the palace, and they drove through one to the right of the impressive main entrance, into a courtyard that had another fountain, more guards and a lot of perfectly maintained greenery in pots.

A quick glance showed all the things Phoebe might have expected—pale stone walls, columns, domed roofs, arched windows, small balconies, abundant flowers growing in pots. It was just as exquisite inside the palace walls as outside. The car drew to a stop by a set of six shallow steps that led to a double set of extra tall doors. When the driver opened her door, she found it took a moment for her legs to cooperate, but she forced herself to step out of the vehicle, even when her palms were sweaty.

'This way, ma'am.'

The driver gestured for her to precede him, and as she walked up the stairs, one hand on the cool metal railing, the doors swung inwards, held that way by two maids in old-fashioned uniforms.

'Thank you.' She smiled tightly, her heart rabbiting in her chest.

Twins.

Her knees knocked.

The guards' vision remained focused straight ahead, almost as if she hadn't spoken. The inside of the palace was overwhelming, but Phoebe barely noticed any of the details. She was conscious of snatches—burgundy carpet, high ceilings, dark wood panelling, enormous flower arrangements that were as fragrant as they were over the top, but her pulse was rushing through her body and her stomach felt so huge and visible, and she knew that in a matter of moments she'd have to explain all of this to Octavio when she was still unpacking it herself.

It was a conversation she'd thought she would have one day, down the track, when she was safely on the other side of the world and he'd married and produced an heir with his perfect princess bride.

And Sasha *was* perfect.

Phoebe had tortured herself by searching the other woman online and had wanted to poke out her eyes afterwards.

They walked through the entrance and down a gallery lined with the kind of art that would have been at home in the Louvre, turned left, so she had a view of the courtyard through one set of windows and the ocean the other, and then, at a set of wide timber doors, the driver paused. A woman stood outside, wearing a suit. They held a low, hushed conversation, and then the woman nodded, knocked once on the doors and stepped inside.

Phoebe exhaled slowly, her body trembling. She trained her attention on the view of the ocean, imagining herself on one of the boats bobbing far out to sea, rather than here, about to have one of the most important conversations of her life.

'Miss James? His Majesty will see you now.'

Phoebe's heart was pounding so hard it hurt. She nodded once, aware that her face must have been incredibly pale. She surreptitiously lifted one hand and pinched her cheeks before she began to walk towards the doors and then, through them.

And she froze.

Because if Octavio had wanted to choose a venue for this conversation that would throw off her ability to concentrate, that would overwhelm her with his power and importance in this country, he'd succeeded completely. She'd expected an office or a sitting room or a *room* of some sorts, not a palace within a palace, but that's exactly what she was looking at. The floors in here were pure white marble, the walls at least twice as high as in the corridor, the chandeliers hanging from the ceiling were crystal, and the walls had intermittent panels that she suspected were actual gold. The windows were enormous, and because the room was at the corner of the palace, the views were stunning in all directions. The furniture was old and beautiful, and in here there were many, many potted plants, all fragrant and glossy green.

And in the centre of the enormous room stood King Octavio, dressed in a black suit, with eyes that were even darker.

The door shut behind Phoebe, and his obsidian gaze seemed to intensify. 'You're pregnant.'

The words were laced with accusation. What could she say? 'Yes.'

'The baby is mine?'

Babies. Babies.

She thought about denying it—panic made her cling to that choice. Wouldn't that be the easiest way out? After all, how could he know she hadn't been sleeping with a whole host of men at around the same time?

'If you deny it,' he forewarned grimly, 'I will arrange a paternity test.'

She gasped. 'I—wasn't going to deny it.'

'Liar,' he said, but softly, as if he was goading her.

She closed her eyes, feeling at a complete disadvantage. Feeling weak, too, and exhausted after the shocking news she'd received that day. 'Can I sit down?'

She blinked over at him to see his eyes narrow, and a muscle jerk in his jaw. He wanted to deny her that. To punish her. He was furious. She could read it all in his face. But he gestured towards a bank of plush sofas, covered in a gold and lavender fabric. 'Go ahead.'

She walked a little unsteadily to an armchair and sat on the very edge of the seat. Hardly a relaxed pose but at least she knew her legs weren't going to give way again.

'I hardly know what to say to you,' he muttered, tone scathing. 'It's true, we barely knew each other, but I thought, I believed—though perhaps it was wishful thinking—that you were a decent person with some kind of moral compass. And yet, now I learn that you were intending to have my baby and what? Never tell me?'

Her jaw dropped at his rendering of events. 'That's oversimplifying things,' she said, fidgeting with her fingers. 'I couldn't tell you.'

'Why not?'

'Putting aside the practical reasons—like I had no way of contacting you and you're not exactly an easy person to reach out to—you were abundantly clear about where your life is headed and what you need from it. You're getting married to a princess, you're going to have perfect royal babies. I'm a cleaner you're ashamed to be seen with. Hello…? What was I going to do? Ruin your life by telling you that somehow we conceived on a night when neither of us ever planned to see the other again?'

He ground his jaw. 'The first night?'

'Yes.' The scan today had confirmed the dates as well.

He grimaced. 'The day of Rodrigo's death.'

She'd thought of that, too. She nodded once.

'So what was your plan?' He returned to his questioning, his voice cold.

'I barely had a plan.'

'You chose not to tell me about the baby,' he pointed out.

Babies, she wanted to scream.

'So then what?'

'I—I'm going to go home. To New Zealand,' she whispered.

His face was carefully blanked of emotion but something stirred in the depths of his eyes. 'I see. And then what?'

'Then I'd take care of… I'd…never bother you again.

You're free to keep going with your life, just as it's been planned out for you.'

'Were you ever going to tell me about the baby?'

'Of course I was,' she said. 'I've spent my whole life not knowing who my father is, there's no way I'd inflict that on another soul.'

He took several steps closer, then thrust his hands onto his hips. It drew her attention to his taut physique. She had to look away again quickly.

'When were you going to tell me?'

'Eventually.'

'I don't believe you.'

She bit into her lower lip, then stopped when his eyes dropped to the gesture.

'When you were married,' she whispered. 'And had a baby—a royal heir.'

He let out a slow breath, dragged one hand through his hair and then cursed. 'You're serious?'

'It seemed best for everyone.'

'Best for our baby not to know me?'

She flinched. She hadn't expected him to feel that way.

'That is my child,' he gestured towards her, 'and that child is a Prince or Princess of Castilona. Their place is here.'

Her skin paled. It was everything she'd been most afraid of—that he would take her baby and raise him or her with his perfect princess wife. But now there were *two* babies to consider. She dropped her head a moment, sucking in air.

'Our babies' place is with me,' she struggled to say.

Silence crackled in the room. She waited on tenterhooks for him to say *Yes, of course*. To say *anything* that would calm her anxiety. But he held the silence, simply staring at her until her stomach was in too many loops to function.

'When did you find out?'

She closed her eyes on a wave of feeling. 'Does that matter now?'

'When?' His response was taut, flattened by stress.

What was there to gain from obfuscating? 'A couple of days after the last time…'

He swore again. 'That's *six weeks* ago.'

Yes. Six long, lonely weeks. She ignored the traitorous thought.

'And you didn't once think it would be appropriate for me to know I had helped to conceive a child?'

'I've explained that. After the way you spelled out your life's plans, how could I think you'd want to know about this? It would ruin everything for you.'

'That was not your decision to make.'

'Given that I was the only one who knew about the pregnancy, it was precisely my decision. And I did it *for you*. For your life, for your future, your family's position in the country, for all the things you made so abundantly clear mattered most to you. Why should a meaningless fling lead to a lifetime of consequences for you?'

'But it should for you?'

She floundered.

'I—am not royal,' she said after a beat. 'I am not betrothed to some prince. I'm a free agent, and while being a single mum is definitely not what I had planned for my life, it's not like I have other plans that this is getting in the way of.' Her voice cracked a little, because she was so close to admitting how off the rails her life had become. The breakdown of her relationship with Christopher had shaken her off-track, and then not being able to find her father had made it all so much worse. She felt completely alone in life, and now she wasn't. Her hand curved over her belly, connecting with the little lives in there.

'Are you telling me this decision was purely altruistic? That no part of your choice came down to the fact you were insulted by my proposal that day?'

'That was not a proposal, it was a proposition, and it was disgusting. But as angry as I was with you, that didn't guide my decision-making.'

'I don't believe you.'

'That's your prerogative. It doesn't matter. None of this matters.'

'It matters a hell of a lot to me. You should have told me.'

She swallowed past a lump in her throat. 'Well, would you like me to tell you something now, Octavio?' She felt her sanity slipping. She felt the shock of that day all mounting up inside of her, forming a wall that was hard and cold yet cracking all over. 'News that will really give you something to shout about?'

His nostrils flared. She knew she should stop, take a breath, try to calm down but her blood was firing at the unfairness of all this. How dared *he* be angry with *her*? 'The hospital director insisted on me getting a full check-up today.' She stood then, needing to feel at more of a level with him. 'I had my first scan.'

Something shifted in his expression. Emotion. Feeling. 'I should have been there.'

'Oh, yes, of course. Because that would have caused

no scandal whatsoever.' She rolled her eyes in a childish gesture that felt wonderful in that moment.

'And?' he demanded, voice like ice.

'And what?'

'The baby is fine?'

'Oh, the baby is fine. In fact, both babies are fine,' she snapped, almost maniacally now. 'It's twins,' she added, and then she sobbed, lifting a hand to her mouth to stop the torrent of emotion from pouring out in a large wail.

Silence cracked around them but she barely noticed. She was shaking now, processing the truth of the scan, the reality that lay before her.

'Well, then.' His voice was low and silky, as though she hadn't just told him they were going to have *two babies* in a matter of months. 'That makes our decision even easier.'

'What decision?' she asked, whirling around to face him. Did he think she was going to have an abortion? Her skin paled and she looked for something to grab hold of, landing on the edge of a large bronze pot.

'There is no way on earth you are leaving the country whilst pregnant with my children, so forget about returning to New Zealand.'

She flinched. She hadn't expected that.

'Nor will my children be born under a cloud of illegitimacy.'

Her heart almost stopped beating; his words made no sense. 'I—don't—what are you saying?'

'That you must marry me—and quickly.'

His words were issued so calmly, with a matter-of-factness that almost seemed to present them as a *fait accompli*, implying she had no say in the matter, that there was no room to negotiate. But of course that wasn't the case. Of course she could choose what she wanted.

'I won't marry you.' She was pleased to have spoken so emphatically.

'That is no longer a choice for either of us.'

'Don't be absurd. Last time I checked, I had free will...'

'But you are pregnant with my twins, and I am the King.'

In the back of her mind, Phoebe wondered how many shocks she could endure in one day. 'So? You might be a king but you cannot force me to marry you.'

'That is true, but there is no court in this land that would award you parental rights over me.'

She gasped.

'Are you saying you'd actually fight me for our babies?'

His nostrils flared. 'That is the very last thing I would want to do.'

'But you'd do it.'

'If you refuse to be reasonable.'

Her eyes swept shut. 'Are you hearing yourself? What you're suggesting is the definition of unreasonable.'

'It's the definition of necessary,' he corrected. 'I know it is far from what either of us wants, Phoebe. I know that. But from the moment you conceived our twins, any other path was closed to us.'

She shook her head, wanting with all her heart for that not to be true.

'I can't marry you,' she groaned, dropping her head into her palm. 'I can't.'

'Why not?'

'Because we're not—we don't know each other. We don't love each other. I don't even *like* you. Scratch that, I loathe you. What kind of marriage would that be?'

'A perfect one, in my book.'

Her jaw dropped.

'Loathing me is not ideal, but I have never sought a typical marriage. My role as King is everything to me—my marriage was always going to be about an heir. That is what I need most right now, and here you are, almost halfway to giving me not one but *two*.'

'Not giving you two,' she snapped. 'Giving birth to them.'

'Unimportant semantics.'

'Not to me.'

'Our marriage can be whatever you wish,' he continued in the same vein, as though she had no say in this. 'You would have some official duties but on the whole you could carve out a role for yourself that was as visible or not as you choose.'

'Gosh, how accommodating you're being,' she muttered sarcastically. 'You're a paragon of reason.'

He expelled a rough breath. 'What do you want me to say, Phoebe?'

'I don't want you to say anything. I don't want *anything* from you.' Her nostrils flared. 'Six weeks ago you walked out of my apartment and as far as I was concerned, I never wanted to see you again.'

'So this pregnancy changed nothing for you?'

'The pregnancy changes everything for me,' she contradicted sharply. 'But none of that concerns you.'

'How are you erasing me from our babies' life?'

'You erased yourself,' she reminded him. 'You made

it abundantly clear how unsuitable I was to be anything more than your secret, shameful mistress.'

'So like I said, this was about punishing me? Because you were offended by the pragmatic and realistic nature of my proposal?'

She stared at him. 'Are you listening to me? You wanted to hide me away back then and now you're saying we should get married. How would that work? You said no one would accept me as your mistress. But they will accept me as your wife?'

'It won't be straightforward,' he said, voice steady. 'You are not who I am expected to marry.'

She stood up then, anger coursing through her veins, and she was so relieved to feel it, because it was easier to manage than anxiety and nervousness. 'You really are a gigantic horse's ass.'

'That,' he enunciated clearly, 'is precisely the kind of thing you will be expected *not* to say when you are Queen.'

The world tilted. Everything went hazy.

She stared at him, aghast.

Queen.

Not just his wife, but Queen of Castilona. She pressed a hand to her stomach, moving towards one of the windows that framed a view over the city and towards the ocean. She stared at the glittering water, made to look almost magical by the way the sun bounced off its surface. This was an ancient and storied kingdom. Its royal family was one of the oldest surviving in the world. There was so much history here, so much tradition. And he was asking her to be a part of that. To be Queen.

She had never sought the limelight though. If anything, Phoebe was shy, and the thought of living her life so publicly sent a chill through her spine. But what did that matter? Octavio was right. Their babies would be princes or princesses of this kingdom, if he chose to acknowledge them as such. That would mean their lives would be public, their role in the line of succession ensuring they were always persons of interest to the public. There was no way Phoebe could let that happen without her being there to protect them. If Octavio was determined to do this, then Phoebe had to be a part of the deal.

But...

Surely she could change his mind?

'This doesn't make sense,' she said with a small shake of her head. 'You're meant to be marrying a princess, and I'm meant to be going home in a few months.'

'This is your home now.'

Something tugged at her heart. Hadn't she felt that way the moment she'd landed? Hadn't the air and the sea and history and architecture weaved in and out of her DNA, reminding her of something she'd never even known? The first time she'd gone to the beach and the water had washed over her bare feet, she'd felt almost as if she were being baptised. It had been remarkable—inexplicable. But that was a connection to her father's homeland; it didn't matter right now.

She glanced at him and then looked away again quickly, when just the sight of him made her pulse tremble.

'What about Sasha?' There was no sense pretending she didn't remember the other woman's name.

'She'll be surprised,' he conceded. 'But not disappointed.'

'You sound convinced of that.'

'We are not a couple.'

Phoebe nodded slowly. 'Still, it might prove embarrassing to her.'

'Unfortunately, that's unavoidable. We were not officially engaged, however. It's only rumours, and they can easily be countered.'

Phoebe's lips pulled to the side. 'This is a lot,' she said, rubbing her temple gingerly. 'I think we should both go and think about this overnight.'

'You may go and think, but it will change nothing for me.'

Her jaw dropped in the face of his absolute certainty, but at least he was offering her a reprieve. She thought longingly of the apartment she'd rented, and the space it would afford her to come to grips with this development.

'Okay.' She lifted one shoulder. 'We can talk tomorrow.'

'Fine. My aide will take you to my apartment.'

Her eyes widened. 'Your apartment?'

'So you can think.'

'I…can think at my place.'

'Impossible.'

'What?'

'You live here now.'

Her jaw dropped at his heavy-handed presumptuousness. 'Octavio, perhaps you're forgetting that I am my own person with an ability to make my own choices in life?'

'I'm not forgetting that.'

'Then stop acting like a bull in a china shop. I'm going back to my apartment where I can think *clearly*.'

'Your apartment is now empty.'

Her heart twisted. 'What?' The whisper was barely audible.

'My security guards have brought your things here. Or rather, they're in the process of bringing them.'

She glared at him, utterly infuriated. 'You had no right to do that.'

'You're going to marry me, and soon. The sooner the better, in terms of your acceptance by the people of Castilona.'

'I'm not going to marry you,' she shouted, her heart racing at the very thought.

'Then you're going to stay here until the babies are born. After that, you may do what you want. It would make things a hell of a lot easier for me, and our children, if you would at least marry me before then, though. Castilonian succession laws are somewhat outdated, you see.'

The colour faded from her skin. She could feel it seeping from her, like tea might stain a mug of boiled water. 'Stop doing that.'

He arched a brow.

'I'm going to be wherever my babies are.'

'Our babies are heirs to the throne of Castilona. They're going to be here.' He enunciated every word of that last sentence with perfect gravity.

Her heart sank to her toes. His proposal seemed almost inevitable, and she hated that. She hated *him* for that. But she also felt something else—something a little like relief. Even though she was furious with Octavio, what he was offering was the kind of safety net she couldn't have imagined, at least materially.

All of Phoebe's life, she'd watched her mother struggle and worry and fret. Money had always been tight, and Phoebe had known her mother had wanted, so badly, to give Phoebe more than she could. She'd wanted her little girl to have so much more, but they'd never been able to afford anything, and in the end, Phoebe had left school at sixteen to get a job, to help pay the rent. When her mother had died, Phoebe had been just seventeen, and everything had fallen apart. No wonder Christopher had been able to draw her into his web so easily. She'd been so alone and so intensely vulnerable, floundering with no idea where she was going in life. He'd come along and swept her up, all handsome and charismatic, and she'd believed his act: hook, line and sinker.

At least Octavio wasn't lying to her. He wasn't trying to charm her into this marriage. Heck, he could have kissed her and got her to agree to just about any damned thing he wanted. But he was laying it all out—what he needed, what he would do if she didn't agree, and what she'd get in exchange.

Yet it still felt like a pathway lined with danger for Phoebe. After all, he held all the cards in this scenario, and she held none. 'I need to think,' she muttered, barely looking at him.

'Then go and think. We'll discuss it further over dinner.'

A shiver ran the length of her spine, because that wasn't an invitation.

'Fine.' She stalked towards him now, her back ramrod straight. 'I hope you know what a bastard you're being.'

He glared back at her, his eyes like coal. 'As opposed to you, who decided to hide this pregnancy from me?'

Her lips parted on a swell of outrage but tears sparkled in her eyes because he had a point. She didn't have any interest in seeing things his way, but if she had wanted to, she could understand how angry he must have been at her. 'Oh, go to hell,' she snapped, stalking from the room and wishing she never had to see him again.

Go to hell? Go to hell? Did she have any idea that he had been plunged into that very state this afternoon?

Seeing her again had been instantly terrifying, because his body had rejoiced on a cellular level, and in that very instant, he'd had to admit to himself how woefully inadequate his attempts had been to forget her, to tell himself she meant nothing to him.

Even if it was just a physical thing, he was still attracted to her in a way that had a horrifying power to fell him to his knees. He accepted then that he could never see her again. He would run a mile over steaming hot coals before he'd open the door to anyone with that power over him.

And a millisecond later, he'd seen that she was pregnant, and a rush of comprehension had dawned on him, like a single bomb at first and then a whole series of them, detonating one after the other as the future he had carefully mapped out and made his peace with was blown to smithereens.

The only future he now saw included Phoebe: the one person he suspected he should never, ever be in the same room with again.

CHAPTER SIX

THE CITY GLITTERED beneath them, an impressive panorama of ancient buildings with golden lights making it look like something from a fairy tale. The moon, full, round and shiny, was high in the sky, bathing them in a lustrous light. The terrace of his apartment in the palace overlooked a private rose garden, and the flowers were heavy with blooms, filling the air with a sweet fragrance. Or perhaps that was the night-flowering jasmine vine that scrambled up the side of the palace and across the stone balustrades? The table had been set for two, decorated with candles and flowers, like some kind of romantic restaurant. Romance, though, was the last thing on either of their minds.

Phoebe had changed into a pair of jeans and a tee-shirt—as Octavio had unceremoniously announced, all her worldly possessions had indeed been invasively handled by his staff and brought to the palace shortly after she'd returned. Though it hadn't been the fault of any of his security team, she couldn't help but glare at them as they carried her goods into the luxurious suite and began to unpack. 'I can do that myself!' she'd exclaimed with heat in her cheeks.

How could she ever get used to living like this?

Phoebe wasn't someone who wanted another person to do her bidding. She wasn't comfortable with the idea of being waited on. She'd taken care of herself—and then her mother—for as long as she could remember.

Dinner was no different. The moment she sat down, a servant appeared to place a napkin across her lap, and another poured sparkling water into her glass, while a third explained the meal to them. Octavio barely batted an eyelid, showing how ordinary this was for him. Though she doubted he'd shared a meal with a pregnant ex-lover at the palace before.

He gestured to the food. 'What would you like?'

Her eyes dropped to the dishes. They all looked excellent, but her stomach was too twisty to think of eating. She glanced at the line of servants across the terrace. 'I thought you wanted to talk,' she said between clenched teeth, her lips forced into an approximation of a smile for the benefit of their audience.

He arched a brow in silent enquiry, so she blinked sideways more obviously, indicating the staff.

'Ah.' Octavio nodded once, then turned to the uniformed group. 'Leave us.'

Two simple words and they began to file away in a perfectly formed line.

'Better?'

Her lips pulled to the side. 'Marginally, but that's not saying much.'

He didn't respond. 'Tell me, how did your thinking go?'

She swallowed past a lump in her throat, reached for her drink and took a sip. 'I don't want to marry you.'

His eyes flashed to hers, so she lifted a hand to forestall anything he might say.

'But I understand why you feel it's necessary.'

He was silent.

Phoebe looped a finger around a clump of hair, twisting it over her shoulder as she searched for the right words. 'I don't want to do this alone.' She bit into her lip. 'I mean, I don't particularly want to do it with you either, but I have to admit, there's something appealing about knowing I'll have support. Even if it's just this.' She gestured to the palace. 'I mean, not having to worry about paying rent and buying food and getting a job when the babies are still young...'

'You would never have to worry about any of these things,' he confirmed slowly.

She massaged her lip with her teeth. 'My mother was alone. Money was always tight. It's hard. I've seen it, I've lived it. I know it's not exactly the best reason to agree to marry someone, but at the same time, it's not the worst reason. You can offer our babies something I never could. I don't think it would be right to turn my back on that.'

He sat back in his chair, watching her without speaking.

'And if you weren't the King, I'd fight you on the necessity of marriage. Lots of people raise kids together and don't get married. We could work out a way to do exactly that.'

'For me, that is not possible.'

'I just said I understand that,' she replied sharply.

He took a sip of his water.

'So, let's talk about it.' Her voice was tentative, thoughtful.

'Aren't we doing precisely that?'

She shook her head. 'I mean our wedding, our marriage. Talk to me about how it would all work.'

'The wedding is not something you need to think about. The palace would organise everything. You only need to show up, repeat the right lines, sign on the dotted line and it's done.'

Her heart turned cold. 'Wow. That's every little girl's dream right there.'

'Did you dream of a big white wedding, Phoebe?' he asked, and the question lacked the acerbity she'd become used to from him.

'I—' Once upon a time she had. Her eyes flitted sideways. 'Is it possible that my personal life isn't going to end up in the tabloids?'

'Not even remotely possible, no.'

'So you might as well hear it from me. I was engaged.'

Surprise flashed across his features. 'That's not ideal, but we can cope.'

'Okay, for starters, that's incredibly hypocritical, given that up until a couple of hours ago you were also planning to marry someone else. And secondly...it gets worse.'

He made a noise that might have been a garbled half-laugh and might have been a groan. 'Of course it does. Go on.'

'My fiancé was married to someone else.' Her voice was so calm, so cold, even though she was telling him something that had shattered her into a billion tiny pieces. 'They had two babies during the three years we were together. I had no idea, obviously.'

He swore softly under his breath, his eyes scanning hers, and for a moment—the briefest of moments—he was human again, not some angry royal automaton trying to manoeuvre her into a cold marriage of convenience.

'You really didn't know?'

She stared at him, aghast. 'Do you honestly need to ask that?'

'I don't know. I don't know you. I thought I did, but this—' He gestured to her stomach.

She angled her face away, frustration coursing through her. 'How dare you?'

'I'll take that as a no.'

'I had absolutely no idea. I thought he loved me. I was planning the damned wedding.' She shivered. 'I thought I'd found my Prince Charming, and my life was finally, finally going to work out. I was wrong.' Another shiver.

She didn't see the emotions that flitted across his face, nor the way a hand tightened into a fist in his lap.

'How did you find out?'

'That doesn't matter. It's not likely to come out.'

'Does anyone else know?'

'Well, my ex, for one.'

'He's not likely to reveal this to anyone. Who else?'

'I don't know. I didn't tell anyone the reason we broke up, but I told people we were engaged. So that's probably going to get out there, and after that, it's not hard to unpick the rest of it. God, I should probably tell him this first, so he has time to prepare his wife.'

'You are seriously thinking of how to mitigate that bastard's inconvenience after what he did to you?'

'Not for his sake, but for his wife's. She was just as innocent as I was.'

He swore. 'Ignore them. They don't matter to you. If

his wife wakes up and realises what he's like, then he will have to deal with it, and she'll be better off.'

Phoebe's stomach swirled.

'What else?' His voice was gruff.

'What do you mean?'

'Is there anything else I should know? Anything that will hit the papers and read like a scandal?'

'Anything else that makes me a liability, you mean?' she enquired sharply, and then sighed. 'This is so far from what you imagined, isn't it?'

'Yes.'

Her heart dropped. 'I bet you wish we'd never met.'

She'd said the words flippantly, but the longer the silence stretched between them, the more she realised she needed him to contradict her. She needed him to reassure her.

And he did, finally, but not as Phoebe wanted. 'I'll never wish that. For a long time, the order of succession has plagued me, and now this. Within months, two legitimate heirs will be born. Believe it or not, apart from having to sort out some logistics, this is good news for me.'

It was nothing to do with Phoebe and it was nothing to do with their babies as people, it was all about the power-brokering and importance of an heir to the King.

'Great,' she said, the word dripping with sarcasm. 'Well, that's pretty much the only scandal in my life. Everything else has been squeaky clean. But you were right that day... I'm definitely not someone who's been groomed in any way whatsoever to become a queen.'

'We can take care of that. You'll undertake lessons here—in protocol, history, languages, politics. By the time the babies arrive, you'll be every bit as regal as if you were born a princess.'

Her heart was heavy with hurt.

She wasn't good enough for him. He wasn't the kind of man to take her, just as she was. He wanted to change her, to improve her, to make her more suitable for him and this role. She'd been a cleaner and he'd used her for sex, he'd propositioned her for more sex, and now he was trying to turn a sow's ear into a silk purse. He was expecting her to play a part, to sell this. At least, that's what it felt like to Phoebe.

She tried not to show how offended she was, but she knew her eyes were likely awash with pain. If he saw it, he didn't say anything to ease the feeling.

'I have two press releases to show you.'

She went very still. Octavio pulled a couple of pieces of paper from his pocket and slid them across the table. Phoebe picked them up and read the first one:

While I understand the temptation to create rumours around long-standing friendships, I am now reiterating the fact that His Majesty Octavio de la Rosa and I are nothing but friends, brought together by our parents' closeness. In fact, I would like to be the first to congratulate him on his impending marriage. I have never seen him so happy, and I wish him and Miss James all the very best.

'From Sasha,' he explained needlessly.

Phoebe flicked to the second statement.

His Royal Highness King Octavio de la Rosa is de-

lighted to announce his engagement to Miss Phoebe James. Their relationship has been conducted in private, and earlier this week the decision was made to marry.

They are also delighted to announce that they are expecting twins, due late in the Autumn.

The couple asks that their privacy be respected at this joyous time.

She stared at the words until they made sense. There was just enough there to make it seem plausible that this was a love match—that their twins had been conceived and their relationship was one of several months rather than three nights—before the truth about her pregnancy came out, as surely it would.

She pushed the papers back towards him, nausea rising in her belly.

'When would these go out?'

'Our social media channels would push them at the same time—tomorrow afternoon. That gives us a chance to have an official portrait taken first.'

She groaned. 'An official portrait?'

'Without it, the press will be clamouring for whatever they can get their hands on. That could be anything from anyone. Let's remove as much of that as possible and simply provide an image.'

Phoebe's gut rolled. 'This is really happening, isn't it?'

'Apparently.'

'You sound about as thrilled as I feel,' she whispered, tears sparkling on her lashes. After several beats of silence, she shook her head forlornly and said, 'God, what a mess.'

* * *

He didn't answer her. He couldn't. He sure as hell couldn't contradict her. This was a royal mess and of their making. He wanted to be gentle with her, to sympathise with her predicament, but whenever a tendency like that came to him, he quashed it.

She had known about this pregnancy for six damned weeks. Six weeks in which she'd contemplated telling him and dismissed the idea. For his sake. Six weeks in which she'd made the cold, calculated decision that he wouldn't be a part of his babies' lives, until it suited her. Weeks and weeks in which she'd decided, every day, that she would deny their babies their birthright and run far away from him.

How dared she?

How dared she think she had any right to do that? And after her own childhood and the absence of her father! Sure, she had said she planned to tell Octavio at some point, but he had only her word for that. What if she'd gone back to New Zealand, met someone else and decided it was just easier to raise the babies with them?

Every iteration made him seethe, and worse was the fact this had all come about by happenstance. If he hadn't gone to the hospital today, he would probably never have seen her again. And he couldn't live with that possibility. It wasn't about Phoebe, but the twins she carried, the babies that he had every right to know and raise as his own children, to raise as his heirs.

He wouldn't forgive her for what she'd almost taken from him, and he doubted he'd ever trust her.

But even when he felt like that, he still hated seeing her suffer. He hated knowing he was the cause of her pain, and he hated knowing that they would never recover from this. He could never forgive her for planning to keep the babies a secret from him, and she would never forgive him for strong-arming her into this marriage.

Their chemistry was as palpable as ever. Desire was whipping him, practically forcing him to reach for her, to obliterate her anxiety the only way he knew how: kiss by kiss by kiss...

'You seriously mean for us to share a room?' Her voice was unnaturally high-pitched, but she couldn't quell it.

'You're expecting me to believe that's a problem?'

'Yes, it's a problem! God, Octavio, we're not a couple!' She lowered her voice to a whisper, even though they were alone. 'We don't like each other, we're sure as hell not sleeping together.'

He arched a dark brow and her irritation grew.

'You can't expect me to find you attractive after the day we've had?'

His laugh was soft and throaty. 'Careful, *querida*. You know how I like to react when you bait me with obvious lies.'

Her jaw dropped. 'I am *not* lying, you...you...' But she floundered, trying to find the perfect way to describe him. 'I am so mad at you.'

'Be that as it may, tomorrow our engagement will be announced to the world. You had better get used to the fact this marriage is happening.'

'This marriage is happening for the sake of the twins, nothing more,' she hissed. 'Behind closed doors, I'd prefer to forget you exist.'

His smirk made her fingers itch to slap him, and she'd

never done that in her life. He stepped closer, but didn't touch her—and it was only then that she realised how badly she wanted him to touch her, regardless of what she was saying. Damn her body for its treacherous reactions to him!

'Let me know how you go with that, won't you?'

'You are unbelievably arrogant.'

'Not arrogant,' he corrected, the humour slipping from his tone. 'Honest. I am furious with you, Phoebe. Angrier, perhaps, than I've ever been with another person, and that's saying something. But I still want you. I'm not afraid of accepting that reality—when you're ready to do the same, I'll be here.'

She glared at him, her nostrils flaring as she expelled an angry breath. 'I guess that leaves me to go find a guest room,' she threw at him, before turning and stomping down the corridor of his incredibly luxurious apartment.

'Stop.' His voice arrested her in her tracks. 'There is no guest room.'

She whirled around to face him. 'What?'

'This is my apartment. I have a study, a gym and a bedroom. Why would I want a guest room?'

She floundered. 'Then in the palace...'

'Yes, there are many bedrooms in the palace, but that's not appropriate.'

Her jaw dropped.

'We are pretending to be in a whirlwind love affair, so madly passionate that we became engaged only months after meeting. I cannot have the veracity of that questioned.'

'Questioned by whom?'

His expression darkened. 'By anyone who would seek to challenge me.'

'Challenge you?' Her brows knit together. 'What do you mean?'

'You take the bedroom. If you're so determined that you can't control yourself around me, I'll take the couch.'

Two pink dots appeared on her cheeks. 'That's *not* what I meant.'

'Of course it is. You don't want us to sleep together, fine. But that's no reason not to share a bed. The bed— by the way—is huge. Easily large enough for us to each take a side. But you know that the minute we're lying down and within arm's reach, something will happen, because we both still want one another. I'm the only one who's game to admit it though. So take the bed, I'll take the couch, and when you accept the reality of our situation, let me know.'

She wanted to fight him. She wanted to scratch him and push him and shout at him, but in the end, she was getting what she wanted. She wasn't even going to feel sorry for him, having to curl his huge frame onto a sofa for the night.

'Okay.' She smiled with exaggerated sweetness. 'Goodnight then, Your Majesty.'

'Sweet dreams…'

CHAPTER SEVEN

LEAVE IT TO Octavio to get the last word in. Sweet dreams, indeed. Not only had she *not* slept remotely well, she'd also been tortured all night. By dreams and memories, by thoughts of their future, by the bed in which she tried to sleep, by the lingering fragrance of him, by the weird temptation to go padding out into the lounge area and watch him sleep. It was all so unsettling, so destabilising, so she awoke in a terrible mood with every intention of giving him a piece of her mind.

Only to find the apartment empty.

He'd left a note on the marble kitchen benchtop.

> *P—*
> *I had a meeting.*
> *I'll see you at the photoshoot. Try to smile.*
> *O*

She screwed the note up and threw it onto the floor before remembering his strange remark the night before about the necessity of fooling everyone into believing this was real. He'd implied his rule was at stake, and whatever she might think of him personally, she didn't want to cause him any problems there. She retrieved the note, tore it into a dozen pieces, then dropped them into the bin.

Phoebe had managed to eat a piece of dry toast and drink a cup of weak tea when a knock sounded at the door to the apartment and one of the staff members she vaguely remembered from the day before stepped inside.

'Madam, the stylist is here.'

'Stylist?' Phoebe gawked, aware that she looked absolutely awful. Her hair was straggly and her face was pale and wan. Her eyes were sunken, courtesy of a lack of sleep, and she was dressed in an oversized tee-shirt that she liked to sleep in.

'Her name is Marie Domingo. May I send her in?'

'I—' But what could she say? The photoshoot loomed large, and Phoebe was nowhere near prepared for that. It was actually kind of thoughtful of Octavio to have arranged this. 'Yes, okay. Why not?'

A moment later, an elegant woman strode into the room—tall and slim with jet-black hair and darker eyes. 'Madam.' She dipped her head. 'I'm honoured to have been asked to work with you.'

Phoebe grimaced. 'Well, don't count your chickens. I need a lot of work.'

'Nonsense.' Marie waved a heavily bangled hand through the air. 'You are beautiful, just unprepared. This will be easy to deal with.' Phoebe went to stand but Marie shook her head. 'Stay, stay, finish up. It will take us a while to set up, anyway.'

Us? Phoebe thought, bewildered.

'Us' turned out to be a team of about six people. Hairstylists, manicurists and two people whom Phoebe gathered were required to carry various outfits around for

Phoebe to inspect, to take her measurements, squeeze her feet into shoes and ferry whatever food or drink anyone required. It was a whirlwind three hours, in which Phoebe was outfitted, had her face made up, her hair washed, trimmed and styled, her nails painted, and when all of that was done, she spent thirty minutes with Marie looking at bridal dresses.

'A Castilonian designer is preferable, but it's a matter of finding who can arrange a gown within a week. It cannot be off-the-rack, it must be sensational, as befits this fairy-tale romance. Are you happy to leave it with me?'

Phoebe stared at her, totally shocked into silence. 'I… yes, of course.'

'Excellent.' Marie consulted her elegant gold wristwatch. 'I've taken up too much of your time.'

'That's fine. It's not like I have anything else scheduled.'

'Actually—' Marie tapped the side of her phone efficiently '—someone from protocol has been waiting to meet with you. We'll leave you to it.'

'Someone from protocol' happened to be an incredibly intimidating man in his sixties who seemed to carry an encyclopaedic knowledge of Castilona, the royal family, the rituals, histories, priorities and requirements. He spent an hour going through what he deemed to be the most vital—mainly surrounding her etiquette whilst engaging in public duties. 'This is only a photoshoot,' he said with a wave of his hand. 'There'll only be a few people in attendance, so it's a good opportunity to practise.'

By then, Phoebe was feeling woozy with everything she would have to convey. Her walk, her expressions, how to hold her hands and position her feet and legs—

it was all so much to hold in her mind, she felt like she might explode.

It was a relief when the time for the photoshoot finally approached and a staff member could lead her from the apartment, through the palace, out of a side door and down a wide set of stone steps that led to an elegant courtyard overgrown with vines. Dressed in a loose silk blouse with puffy sleeves, and a pair of slim trousers, her belly was barely noticeable, though her breasts felt enormous.

She looked around and saw a photographer was already set up, surrounded by a few assistants who were busy managing the set up and checking lighting levels. Phoebe stared at them, her heart in her throat. She was so engrossed in their activity that she missed the moment Octavio strode out from an entrance to their left, fixing one of his cuff-links in place.

She missed the way his eyes landed on her and stayed there, heavy on her frame, as if he couldn't possibly look away. She missed the way admiration softened his features a moment, parting his lips, and she missed the way he fought to regain his equilibrium. She saw only cynicism on his features when he approached her and she realised he was there.

Phoebe shivered at the expression.

'Ready?' he asked, one brow lifted.

'As I'll ever be.'

'It's a photoshoot, not a form of torture.'

'It's what the photoshoot represents.'

'And what's that?'

'The beginning of the lie.'

'I thought you'd be more than comfortable with lying

by now? After all, six weeks of keeping your pregnancy from me should have made you practised in deceit.'

She wanted to shove him.

Before she could respond, he reached into his pocket. 'Here, put this on.'

She glanced down at his hand expecting—strangely enough—something like a microphone. Instead, he held a small black velvet box. Phoebe made no attempt to take it, so a moment later, Octavio impatiently opened the box and turned it around for her to see. Inside was a beautiful ring, a large solitaire diamond in the middle of a circlet of black diamonds.

'It's…so lovely,' she said honestly, and frustratingly, tears sparkled on her lashes. 'God, I'm going to ruin my make-up.'

He was quiet, his lips pushed together. She reached for the ring, her fingers shaking a little.

'I don't trust myself not to drop it,' she murmured.

With a sound of something like impatience, Octavio removed the ring and took hold of her hand. The moment their flesh connected she felt it—the same thousand little sparks from their first meeting flew through her arm and exploded into a cacophony of fireworks inside her body.

'It was my mother's, and my grandmother's before her.'

'Oh.' Her heart twisted. It shouldn't have made a difference, but somehow it did. Just imagining herself wearing something that was so personally significant felt wrong, given what they meant to each other. 'Are you sure?'

'Yes.'

'But it's obviously very special to you—'

'And my wife, therefore, should have it.'

'But I'm not really—'

'From now on, for all intents and purposes, you are.' He compressed his lips, glanced across at the photographers then back to Phoebe. He drew her closer, close enough that only she could hear his raspy whisper. 'Stop acting like a deer in headlights and remember that in a week's time, you'll be Queen.'

The stylist Marie had also said something about getting a dress in a week but it hadn't quite penetrated the fog of Phoebe's brain. Now she blinked up at Octavio, eyes wide with surprise. 'A *week*?'

'The sooner the better,' he agreed.

'A week.' Phoebe struggled to draw in breath. She pressed a hand to her belly, heart pounding. She could do this. She *had* to do this. She'd agreed, for the sake of their baby, and Octavio's role as King required a certain amount of play-acting. If he wanted her to go out there and sell herself as the doting, loved up Queen-to-be, so be it. He was right—the time for 'deer in the headlights' was over. 'All right. I'm ready.'

His surprise was obvious, his eyes scanning her face as if looking for vestiges of doubt, but there were none. Phoebe had been terrified a moment ago but now, she was ready. She could do this—she had to.

When he'd first seen Phoebe, he'd been mesmerised by her grace. He remembered thinking that she moved as if she were in a ballet. It turned out, she acted like it, too. He was almost rendered speechless by the way she captivated the photographers, charming them with her casual yet intelligent conversation, moving with fluid grace and beauty, smiling in a way that seemed to chan-nel every star in the heavens.

'We'll always share the stars, my darling.'

He pushed his mother's voice from his mind, not want-ing to think about her then. Not wanting to wonder if she'd have approved of the way he'd manoeuvred this marriage or not—because he suspected she wouldn't have.

'Your Majesty, we thought we'd try a photograph of the pair of you standing by the trees here. The pink of the oleander will pick up Miss James's complexion so nicely.'

He glanced across at his bride-to-be and saw what they were saying—her cheeks were sweetly pink, her lips, too. 'Fine.' He sounded gruff and impatient—now who needed help playing a part?

As if to remind him, Phoebe reached down and took his hand. But what might have appeared to be a normal thing for a couple to do was actually a tight squeeze from his fiancée, to prompt him into behaving.

Something twisted in his gut. Frustration. Annoy-ance. *Need.*

Sleeping on the sofa had been almost unbearable. He'd craved her for more than a month and a half, but he'd put up with it. He hadn't even known for sure that she was still in Castilona. But now she was in his palace, in his apartment, just one room away, and he wanted her with a ferocity that almost felled him. Yet he'd stayed on the sofa, hadn't pushed his cause, and he wouldn't. If they were together again, it would be because she asked him. He wasn't going to throw himself at her—he wasn't going to debase himself by risking rejection. Not from Phoebe. He'd known enough rejection in his life, and

he'd survived it, but somewhere deep inside he understood that if Phoebe kept pushing him away it would be
worse somehow.

In front of the trees, he stood as stiff as a board. Little wonder the renowned portrait photographer frowned.
'Could you try a different pose? Just relax. Pretend we're
not here,' she invited with a wry smile.

Phoebe turned around and her own frown echoed the
photographer's. 'You look miserable,' she murmured.

'I'm not.'

'Then why do you look as though you're about to walk
on a bed of nails?'

He flashed her a look and felt a weird tug on his lips.
A half-smile.

'Better,' she said, tilting her head, 'but not quite good
enough.'

She stood on tiptoes, whispering into his ear so only
he could hear. 'I am pregnant with your children and in
less than six months you'll have your heirs. Surely that's
enough to make you smile for a few photos? Remember,
this was your idea.' But she tilted her head after she'd
spoken and a form of madness overtook him, so instead
of just saying he agreed, he angled his own face and
caught her mouth with his, kissing her even though he
hadn't meant to and she hadn't expected it.

Kissing her even though she wore lipstick and they
weren't alone. Kissing her as if he had every right, as if
they were a real couple, as if it was the only path for his
salvation. Kissing her even when he'd vowed to himself
moments earlier that he wouldn't keep putting himself
in a position to be rejected by Phoebe.

He didn't want to be rejected by her.

He pulled away and managed to control his reactions to her, to his body's sharp physical need for her, assuming a mask of control. 'I remember what we're doing, Phoebe—pretending to be a couple in love. Let's just get this over with.' He saw her frown and hated himself as soon as he'd said the words; he saw the hurt in her eyes and wanted to punch something.

He was so angry with her for keeping the pregnancy from him, for what had almost happened. If he hadn't seen her in the hospital, quite by chance, he would never have known about these babies, and that was a reality he could never accept.

And yet she was here and had agreed to marry him. It wasn't fair to continually punish her for a decision she'd made, according to herself, out of a desire to do what was right by him.

He opened his mouth to apologise, but she was already stepping back from him. 'I just need to check my make-up,' she said with a wave of her hand, gliding away from him as though he were a bomb set to detonate.

In the end, the photos they got were excellent. Only Phoebe could see beyond the poses they'd chosen to imitate a happy couple to the lines of tension around Octavio's eyes or the slightly too static line of her own smile. The announcements had predictably set off a feeding frenzy. Octavio had been wrong—sharing a couple of images and a press release hadn't come close to assuaging the interest in their romance. Some staff at the hospital evidently decided it would be more profitable to become royal informants rather than continue working their jobs and had breached *clínica* regulations by professing to be Phoebe's dearest confidants and having all sorts of inside details on the relationship.

Of course, that was false. There had been no relationship, and what she and Octavio had shared had been kept completely private by Phoebe. She'd had no interest in discussing her personal life with anyone. She'd still been reeling from the breakup with Christopher and had learned not to trust anyone with anything.

Phoebe had left school at sixteen, when her mother had become sick and couldn't work. She hadn't really kept in touch with any of those friends and yet a couple of them were also cashing in on their tenuous links to Europe's new soon-to-be queen. Old school photos surfaced on the internet, as well as silly anecdotes about her teen years. 'I always knew she was destined for something amazing. Phoebe's the kind of person who could do anything she wanted in life. She'll make a wonderful queen.' That quote had been from her high school English teacher, and it made her smile. Of all the people who'd been interviewed about Phoebe, Mrs Warwick was the one who had actually known her. She'd pushed her to stay in school.

'You're too bright to walk away from this, Phoebe. You have such potential.'

There were trolls, too. Everyone had opinions on Phoebe, and apparently, she didn't live up to what they saw as Octavio's match. The comments, whether good or bad, were infuriating. She was tempted to throw her phone into the lake that sat perfectly in the south gardens of the palace.

By the fourth day, the palace's PR machine was approaching her about doing an interview.

'The world wants to know about you. If we don't give them the information, they'll fill the void.'

Phoebe wasn't interested in that.

On the fifth day she received a message, out of the blue, from Christopher. It was so unexpected she clicked into it without taking the time to prepare and read his words with a wave of nausea:

Phoebe, we need to talk. Call me. X

She flicked out of the message, with warm cheeks and a sense that she'd done something wrong.

The palace continued to gently question her about doing an interview. She broached the subject with Octavio two nights before their wedding. 'If you want to do an interview, then do one.'

Hardly helpful.

Nor was it helpful that he continued to sleep on the sofa, that he hadn't even suggested joining her in bed since that first night.

To be fair, he was doing exactly what she'd asked him to do, but Phoebe's whole body was screaming for him now, and in the maelstrom of all this, she could only think how comforting it would be to have *him*. To at least have that touchstone to cling to, when everything else felt so wildly out of control. Not that sex with him was *in* control, but it was predictably wild, and reassuringly passionate. It made Phoebe feel alive and in the moment. It made it impossible to think about anything else, to worry, to stress. It was just…good.

But Octavio was acting as though she barely existed. He was in the apartment sparingly, the palace was too huge to run into him, and she gathered he was busy with government matters, meaning Phoebe was left to do her lessons with the private tutors that had been arranged for her, in peace.

Too much peace.

Too much time to scroll her phone and read the comments and articles and predictions and feel like her tummy had been hollowed out.

The worst were the ones that were true. Comments like:

It's obviously just because of the babies. No way would sexy King O marry someone like her except for the pregnancy.

On the morning of the wedding, Phoebe got through the extensive preparations by separating herself from her body. She stood in the middle of the suite as a team of stylists set to work on her hair, skin, make-up, nails, feet. Everything. She extended her arms when they asked her to, pursed her lips, angled her head, whatever they needed she did, and when it was time to slip into the stunning designer gown Marie had arranged for her, she was careful and neat and very still as they fastened the dozens of buttons that ran down the back.

In the fuss of preparations, when Phoebe was ready, the door opened and a beautiful woman with hourglass curves and shiny honey-brown hair sashayed confidently towards Phoebe. She had a kind of beauty that was rare, and unfair to other women. Her skin was soft and supple, youthful, her eyes were stunning in shape and colour, her lips a full, curving line, painted a dramatic red. But she also seemed to glow with kindness. 'Can we have a moment?'

Phoebe knew who she was immediately. This woman had the same innate confidence as her royal cousin—this must be Xiomara, whom she'd heard Octavio speak of a couple of times.

'I'm glad I finally get to meet you,' Xiomara said, when they were alone. 'My cousin is very protective of you.'

'Is he?'

'Oh, yeah. He's been keeping you locked up so you had time to get ready for the wedding. I told him I'd be better at helping you than anyone else, but he disagreed.' Xiomara rolled her eyes. 'You know how insufferable he can be.'

'Oh, I sure do,' Phoebe agreed, liking the other woman immediately.

Xiomara grinned, then studied the bride. 'You look beautiful, by the way.'

'It's all their work.' She gestured towards the closed door. 'I'm just the canvas.'

'Don't be so self-deprecating.'

Phoebe opened her mouth.

'No, I mean it. *Don't.* There's a pack of wolves out there, and they'll eat you alive if you give them the slightest chance. You have to appear confident even when you don't feel it, okay?'

'You're right, you would have been way better at preparing me. What else?'

'Bet you wish you could have some champagne right now, huh?'

Phoebe laughed. 'Actually, I wish I could have a shot

of something stronger, but I'm not even drinking water because I don't want to have to pee again.'

Xiomara grimaced. 'Right. So let's run through the day.'

Xiomara was thorough and so confident that it couldn't help but rub off on Phoebe, and they spent thirty minutes discussing the wedding, the dinner afterwards and the people she should avoid.

'You'll have to meet my father, but take my advice and don't get stuck with him for long. I'll try to manage that for you. The King and he...they don't see eye to eye at all.'

Phoebe nodded.

'One last thing.' Xiomara reached into the small designer clutch she carried. 'Tavi asked me to give you this.'

Tavi. Her heart twisted. What a sweet nickname for a man who seemed far too intimidating to ever have such a thing.

'What is it?'

'No idea, sorry. I'm just the messenger.' She handed over a small velvet pouch. 'Would you like me to leave you in privacy?'

'No, that's fine. It's probably just something... I don't know.' Her fingers trembled a little as she opened the pouch and removed a fine platinum chain on which a locket was suspended. It was dainty, oval shaped and with diamonds inlaid. She ran a finger over them. 'It's beautiful.'

'A locket? What's inside? Don't tell me he's put a picture of himself in there,' Xiomara said on a soft laugh.

Phoebe separated one side of the locket from the other,

hinging it open, and her breath caught in her throat while her heart rammed into her ribs.

'It's my mum,' she whispered, staring at the picture of her mother smiling back at her.

'Oh, God. That's actually really sweet.' Xiomara's arm came around Phoebe's waist, squeezing her. 'She's beautiful.'

'Yeah, she was.' Phoebe blinked back tears. 'I can't cry. My mascara will run.'

'He should definitely have given you that himself,' Xiomara said with a shake of her head.

'It's just so thoughtful of him,' Phoebe said unevenly, her mind spinning. Had he understood how badly she was missing her mother? Not just today, but ever since learning of her pregnancy and feeling so alone on that journey?

A knock sounded at the door. Xiomara looked at Phoebe. 'You ready?'

Phoebe nodded, but tears still sparkled on her lashes.

'Come in,' Xiomara called, then turned back to Phoebe. 'Would you like to wear it?'

'Of course.' She nodded quickly. 'Would you mind helping me?'

Xiomara clasped the necklace in place and Phoebe glanced at the mirror. It was perfect.

Marie entered the room with two guards, one of whom carried a velvet cushion with a diamond tiara on it. Of course there'd been mention of a tiara but stupidly Phoebe had envisaged something small and, well, cheap, something almost for show. But this was quite obviously from a royal vault of some kind, and it was most definitely not small, nor cheap.

'This tiara was commissioned for the King's great-grandmother,' Marie explained. 'It has one hundred and eighty carats of diamonds, a mix of pear and marquise cut, and is set in platinum. It's very, very special and we all think it will look perfect on you. Do you like it?'

Phoebe's jaw dropped. 'Did you say one hundred and eighty carats?'

'Don't think about it,' Xiomara advised quickly. 'Trust the stylish people.' She wiggled her perfectly shaped brows and Phoebe laughed.

'Okay,' she said with a nod. 'Show me.'

She stood still as the team worked their magic, and by the time they were done Phoebe had to admit she definitely looked the part. There was nothing more to do now but act it.

CHAPTER EIGHT

HER DRESS WAS PERFECT. She looked like an angel—and the cut of the fabric almost disguised her pregnancy. At her throat she wore the locket he'd sent with Xiomara, and on her face she had a perfect smile pinned. He knew it was just for show but no one else would, because Phoebe was a damned good actress. She looked serenely beautiful. She looked regal. He couldn't look away—he told himself he was also acting a part, but in that moment he wasn't acting. He was existing. He stared at her because he wanted to. She had been preceded by a collection of bridesmaids, none of them known to Phoebe, all of them from the aristocracy.

When Xiomara approached the front of the church, she winked at Octavio and he relaxed a little.

The ceremony itself seemed to go on for ever. There was so much to get through, so much custom and tradition, and Octavio was conscious of Phoebe beside him and how long she was standing, how much he wished he could put an arm around her waist for support. She wasn't heavily pregnant, and she was fit and young, but he still wanted her to be comfortable.

Finally, it ended, and they were invited to kiss one another.

Octavio's pulse ratcheted up about a thousand degrees. He glanced at Phoebe and saw the same feeling in her face that was bombarding him. Worry.

Because when had they ever kissed and it had not overtaken them?

He leaned down, breathing her in, her fragrance so sweet and familiar that he almost groaned. He wanted her so much it was like a fire raging out of control. If he kissed her, he feared he wouldn't be able to stop. And so instead of giving in to temptation and drawing her against his body, tilting her head back so he had full rein of her mouth, he simply pressed his lips to hers for several seconds, allowing the cameras to snap the moment. She stiffened against him, as if she too was fighting something more, so he knew he'd made the right decision to keep this PG. Rapturous applause broke out and he pulled away, feeling as though he deserved a medal.

'Are you tired?'

Phoebe heard the question and tried not to think there was any concern for her in his tone. He was asking because of the pregnancy. 'Yes,' she answered honestly, smothering a yawn. Were queens allowed to yawn? She was glad she'd changed from her bridal gown and tiara into a simple cream suit—it would be much quicker and easier to strip out of, making it faster to get into bed. She was exhausted.

'Then we should go.'

'Oh, it's fine.' She shook her head once. 'The party's still going.'

'It will continue without us. It's after midnight. It's time.'

'After midnight? Already?'

'I'm glad to hear you've been enjoying yourself.'

She wouldn't exactly say that. The whole night, Phoebe had been in demand. Every dignitary, member of the aristocracy and anyone in between had wanted to speak with her. Her head was swimming with the sheer volume of conversation she'd entered into. From time to time, Xiomara had come to her rescue, and those had been high points of the night for Phoebe. Around Xiomara, she felt strangely relaxed.

Around Octavio, it was the opposite. She braced now as he put his hand in the small of her back and guided her towards a set of double doors across the ballroom.

Phoebe was still getting her bearings in the palace. She didn't think she'd used this access before. Sure enough, it brought them onto a small, terraced area, and beyond it, a car was waiting.

'What's this?'

'Our ride.'

She arched a brow. 'Ride? We live right here. I'm not too tired to walk the few hundred metres to your room.'

'We're not staying in the palace tonight.'

She blinked across at him. 'Why not?'

'Because it's our honeymoon.'

'Octavio,' she said, and her voice trembled a little, 'we don't need a honeymoon.'

He looked at her and the air between them seemed to pulse and hum, to swirl around her with a force that was mesmerising and magnetic. He moved closer and her breath caught in her throat, trapped there by an invisible force. 'It's the way it should be,' he said, his eyes scanning hers, probing them, as if looking for the answer to a question he hadn't posed.

'You mean it's what people will expect?'

His lips quirked in the hint of a frown. 'That, too. Let's go.'

They drove for so long that Phoebe became drowsy and her head fell onto Octavio's shoulder, but she was too tired to sit up again. At one point, half asleep, she murmured to him, 'Thank you for my necklace.'

She was barely conscious of his stiffening beneath her, and he was quiet for so long she thought he might not say anything. Then, he responded, 'It's tradition for Castilonian grooms to gift their brides something on the morning of their wedding. I thought you'd like it.'

Tradition. It probably wasn't even his idea. Octavio was hardly the kind of man to come up with such a thoughtful gift idea and do the legwork of finding a photo of Phoebe's mother, having it printed and set into the locket. And though it was still beautiful, the necklace lost some of its charm for Phoebe then. She'd loved it because of what it was, but also because he'd thought to give it to her. There was an odd heaviness on her chest that made her want to blot everything out.

She fell asleep and at some point woke up with Octavio's arms cradling her against his chest as he carried her from the car. She tried to wake up, to say something else, but she was exhausted in that way pregnancy led to, and it had been a huge day to boot. She surrendered to a wave of sleepiness, and the next thing she knew, she was waking up in an unfamiliar bedroom, staring right out at the beach.

She sat bolt upright, trying to make sense of where she was and with whom, and it all came rushing back to her. The wedding. The locket. The party. The dress. The people. The fact she was now married.

And a queen.

Octavio's wife.

Her heart raced as she looked down at her hand for confirmation and saw two bands there—the stunning engagement ring and a simpler platinum band with several small diamonds set into it.

She reached for her throat and felt the locket, opened it and saw her mother's face and frowned, a maelstrom of feelings rolling through her.

She was alone in this room; she presumed Octavio was somewhere in this place though. It was, after all, their honeymoon.

She grimaced at the idea, because theirs was so far from a normal relationship, but she stood up, realising she was still in the pantsuit she'd been wearing last night. He hadn't even undressed her. Because he hadn't wanted to? Or because he hadn't felt that he had a right?

Whatever.

She was relieved, she told herself, moving from the bedroom and out into a corridor that was light and airy, the walls rendered white, the doorways carved and arched. She scanned the rooms and found him, not in the kitchen, where she'd been heading for her one and only coffee of the day, but rather on the balcony, shirt off, body ridiculously honed and tanned, staring out to sea.

Her mouth went dry.

Her insides squirmed.

And though she made no noise, somehow he must have detected her presence because he turned and looked right at her, so their eyes clashed and her whole body responded with a pulsing, aching need.

She glanced away quickly, her cheeks hot, the ground beneath her seeming trembly. She felt scared.

Scared to be here, alone with him. Scared of what it would mean for her and her ability to resist him. She'd spent a full week longing for him and managing to be strong, but how realistic was it to stick to that?

Would she really spend her whole life ignoring this desire?

Would he?

Did she want to?

Her legs moved of their own volition, across the floor towards the sliding doors and out onto the balcony. The air here was sweet, tinged with the fragrance of the Mediterranean Sea and the greenery that bounded it. There were white and pink Oleander trees forming a border and a heap of lavender scrambled beneath it, growing quite wild. Though not native to the Mediterranean, at some point a heap of palms had been planted around the beach and they gave the impression of being stranded on a tropical island rather than somewhere in Castilona.

'Where are we?' she asked, her voice a little raspy from disuse.

'It's a private beach, not far from Costa de las Estrellas,' he said. 'Do you know it?'

'I've never heard of it, but I love the sound of the name.'

'Coast of the Stars,' he said with a nod, but there was something in his eyes that gave her pause. 'It's a coastal town; an old fishermans' village, but over the years it's become synonymous with good food and wine and some of the best beaches in the world. As a result, it's an exclusive tourist destination. My family has had a holiday home here for a long time. This is our beach.'

'Our beach? You mean it's really private?'

He pointed down the sand in one direction and then the other. She noticed that the Oleander trees had been planted to follow the line of the coast, shielding the beach from view. On each side of the house, there was only vegetation.

'Completely private.'

She let out a low breath. 'So we're alone?'

'A housekeeper is available if we want one, but generally when I come here, it's because I am seeking my own counsel.'

She looked at him thoughtfully. 'Do you come here often?'

'I used to, before the coronation.'

She returned her attention to the beach. It was a warm day and the thought of swimming tugged at her.

'I grew up near the beach,' she found herself admitting. 'In the summer, you'd be hard-pressed to get me out of the water. I loved to surf.'

'That's something we have in common.'

Her hands gripped the railing, tightening around it.

'Where in New Zealand are you from?'

'Not far from Raglan. It's on the North Island.'

He nodded. 'Is that where you were planning to return to?'

She shook her head a little. 'After my mum died, I moved to Auckland. That's where I live now. Where I lived.' She frowned, remembering her old life with a shock. It almost felt like something that had happened to someone else. She thought of Christopher, recalled his text message, felt a hint of guilt for not returning it, but then anger that he'd thought he had any right to contact her.

'Where you met your ex-fiancé?'

Had he been reading her mind?

'Yes.'

'How did you meet him?'

She bit into her lip. 'I was a receptionist at a school, and he was a contractor brought in to run some professional development training for teaching staff. We got talking in the break room one day and…the rest is history.'

'Love at first sight?' he asked, and try as she might, she couldn't detect even a hint of mockery in his question.

She shook her head. 'I thought he was handsome, but I still wasn't over losing my mum. It had been a couple of years by then, but I took it hard. I was struggling. I wasn't ready to be involved with anyone.'

'So how did you get together?'

'He took it slow. He told me he understood. Bit by bit, he got me to open up. To trust him.' Her voice shook with anger. 'And then, to love him. Or to believe I loved him. Looking back, I don't know if it's possible to love someone who's using you like that.'

His finger brushed her shoulder lightly. She turned to face him, and something shifted deep in her soul. Christopher seemed like a thousand lifetimes ago.

'He hurt you.'

'He changed me,' she admitted, tilting her chin a little. 'At the time it hurt, but I'm stronger because of what I went through. I would never trust so easily again. Maybe I'll never trust anyone again,' she amended. 'But if I do, it would take a lot.'

'Not everyone is capable of that kind of deceit. In fact, most people aren't.'

'I don't know,' she said with a lift of one shoulder. 'I don't know if it's worth taking the risk. There were no markers with him. Everything seemed so normal. I had no reason to believe he was already married. What kind of psychopath proposes to another woman when he's married and expecting a baby, and then another, with his wife?'

'A psychopath, like you said,' Octavio agreed. 'You're better off without him.'

'I know that.' She nodded. 'I'm just glad I found out before we went through with some kind of sham marriage ceremony or something. I have no idea how far it would have gone if I hadn't learned the truth.'

'How did you find out?'

'I was out at lunch. Christopher just happened to be at the same restaurant, with his wife, their children and his parents. It was mortifying.'

'You hadn't met his parents?'

'No. He told me they were dead.' Her voice trembled a little. 'I literally ran right into him when I was paying the bill. His wife was beside him, holding their children's hands. Our eyes met and I just knew by the look of mortification in his face, the look of worry and fear that I might out him, that I'd been the Other Woman. He couldn't act like he didn't know me—I'd said his name by then and asked what he was doing there. I hadn't re- alised until it was too late what was going on, so he had to come up with an elaborate lie about how we knew one another, and the penny finally dropped.'

'When was this?'

'About two months before I flew to Castilona.'

'That's not long ago.'

She shook her head. 'I came as quickly as I could pack up my life and get a passport sorted.'

'He's a bastard.'

'Yes.'

His hand moved to her chin, touching it lightly. He looked as though he was concentrating hard. 'You're—' His eyes dropped to her lips, lingered there, and though it was only a glance, it might as well have been a heady, intimate touch, for the way warmth spread through her.

'I'm…?' she prompted, but breathlessly, as though her lungs could hardly fill with air.

He closed his eyes then, the lashes forming thick, dark half moons against his tanned skin.

'Forget it.' His hand dropped away, and when he opened his eyes, determination was visible in their depths. 'I didn't bring you here to seduce you. You have boundaries and I intend to respect them. Let's go get something to eat.'

Phoebe's heart dropped to her toes even as it exploded in her chest.

'You have boundaries and I intend to respect them.'

Then kiss me! she wanted to shout. *Kiss me until my knees are weak and I forget I've ever, ever been hurt! Kiss me because when you kiss me everything makes a terrifying kind of sense, on a fundamental level. Kiss me now; kiss me and keep kissing me.*

But she said none of those things, and Octavio stepped

backwards and then walked in off the deck, leaving Phoebe alone with the fragrant sea-breeze.

'There will be photographers,' he warned, as they approached a sleek black sports car parked out front of the beachy holiday cottage. 'Not specifically for us, yet, but because this town is the kind of place celebrities come. Don't be surprised if there's a lens pointed at you.'

She wrinkled her nose. 'Great. Sounds like fun.'

'You get used to it.'

'Really? Aren't we just going to get breakfast? That's not particularly newsworthy.'

'You'd be surprised.'

She sat in the front passenger seat and before she could do it herself, Octavio was reaching across Phoebe for the seat belt and sliding it into position. His hands brushed her belly and Phoebe's breath hissed between her teeth. She jerked her gaze to his, wondering if he'd felt it. The electric shock. The current of awareness.

'Do you mind if I...' He held one hand towards her stomach.

She shook her head. 'I don't mind. They're your babies, too.'

'But it's still your stomach.'

'Just a home right now,' she said with a shrug.

He pressed his palm to her side and one of the babies kicked immediately. Phoebe laughed, her eyes meeting Octavio's, who looked utterly shocked. 'Was that—a baby?'

'Yes.'

He swore under his breath. Another kick.

'That baby is active. I think they like your touch.'

She had meant it as a simple observation, but she heard the words and wondered how they'd sounded to Octavio. Like an invitation? Did they prove that she was every bit as needy as she actually was?

'Then I might have to touch more.'

'It could be your voice, too,' she murmured.

'Talk, touch. We are here for two more nights—let's experiment.'

Her heart raced. Two nights? It seemed like an eternity and nowhere near enough.

They had to drive through a heavily fortified security gate that was lined on either side by a fence at least four metres high, concealed by overgrown trees but nonetheless menacing and effective. Once through it, on the short road to town, Octavio spoke about the surroundings, the village, making conversation almost as if they were friends. It was so unexpected that when he pulled the car to a stop in the main street of a charming, ancient fishing port, she turned to him and blurted, 'Why are you being so nice to me?'

He frowned a little. 'I don't actually know. I keep reminding myself how mad I am with you, but then, when I'm with you, I find it hard to remember that. I suppose I find myself thinking about the future, and the fact we're having babies and wondering if we shouldn't try to let bygones be bygones, to some extent. If I think about you leaving the country, pregnant with my children, and never telling me the truth, I am furious. And yet, that didn't happen. Maybe it never would have happened; who knows? You're here, we're married, our babies will grow up as my children, my heirs. I have no interest in hating you for the sake of it.'

She let out a long, slow breath.

If only it were that easy.

Maybe it could be?

But when she looked at Octavio, it was impossible not to feel wary. Wary of how he'd hurt her, when he'd asked her to be his mistress. Making her feel as though that was all she'd ever be good for. Reminding her so clearly of how Christopher had made her feel. Breaking her all over again. Not her heart but something more than that—her belief in herself; her essence.

She didn't want to hate him either, but she was afraid to like him too much as well.

But so long as she remembered—remembered *everything*—like how easily Christopher had deceived her, how trusting she'd been. Like how Octavio hadn't been interested in her as a person—not in terms of wanting anything from her beyond sex—before he'd learned about the pregnancy. This was and always would be about the twins; so long as she didn't forget that, she'd be fine. Maybe she could even take a page out of his book and let bygones be bygones...

CHAPTER NINE

THEY SHARED BREAKFAST at an intimate café with views of the water and a small but excellent menu. Phoebe had woken starving and chose a magdalena as well as a frittata, washed down with a glass of orange juice. Afterwards, they walked the main street together. Phoebe glanced in shop windows at first, but as they walked, side by side without touching, she became more and more aware of the attention they were drawing. Not just the handful of photographers Octavio had suggested might be lurking but also regular tourists, all armed with their cell phones, taking photographs and videos and no doubt sharing them online.

It had been a beautiful start to the day, but Phoebe's patience quickly wore thin.

'Shall we get back to the villa?' he asked, as if reading her mind.

She glanced at him gratefully. 'Yeah. I'd like that.'

They drove most of the way in silence, Phoebe frowning a little as she lost herself in thought. After a while though, she turned to face him. 'Do you really get used to it?'

'For the most part.'

'Does that happen often?'

'Pretty much everywhere I go.'

She shook her head. 'It's just so invasive.'

'Mostly it comes from a good place. People are curious about my life.'

'Because you're a king?'

'And because my parents died when I was so young. I was orphaned. There was a lot of sympathy for me.'

She reached across, putting her hand on his knee in a gesture of comfort. She didn't say anything—she didn't need to. They'd discussed grief and loss; he knew how she felt. He knew she was sorry for anyone to suffer in that way.

As they approached, the gates swung open to allow his car to pass through them, and Phoebe expelled a sigh of relief. 'The town is beautiful but I like it here better.'

'I should have known. It's too soon.' He reached across, stroked her cheek as though he couldn't help himself. 'On the other hand, it will further sell our story as being legitimate.'

Phoebe's eyes widened. Was that what breakfast had been about? Had it all been for show? To display her around town, so the press could get images and feed the public's insatiable appetite for news on the royal couple?

She bit back a groan. Hadn't she just been telling herself that so long as she *remembered*, everything would be fine? And instead she'd been swept up in how decent he'd been behaving, treating her like a normal person. She'd forgotten that he was tactical, always thinking about his kingdom, his duties, treating her as anything but a whole, normal person that mattered.

She put her hand on the door the moment he parked, and opened it gratefully, stepping outside and breathing in, trying to anchor herself firmly to reality. But here, in this beautiful place, everything inside of her seemed to be shifting and changing, making it hard to know what she felt and wanted.

He walked closely behind her, and when they were inside he said, 'I'm going to catch up on some work. Take a look around—there's a well-stocked library, a media room with all the streaming services, a gym. Do whatever you want. Just—be careful.' His eyes dropped to her stomach. As if she needed any further reminders that this was all just about the babies!

He resisted the urge—but only just—to lock the door to his office. He'd come so close to reaching out and touching her stomach again, to touching *her*, to drawing her close to him and asking if he could kiss her. He'd wanted to drag her against his body all morning. In town, their hands had brushed as they'd walked. Such an innocent gesture, and yet it had been almost incendiary to Octavio, who felt as though he was burning up with desire for his wife.

But she'd made it obvious she didn't want that. Even when on one level she did, she was determined to avoid it—and him. And he had to respect that. So he buried his head in his work, surprised to find it was mid-afternoon before he looked up and wondered where Phoebe was.

He strode from the office, telling himself he was looking for a late lunch rather than his bride, but when he couldn't immediately see her in the house, worry began to curdle in his gut. He quickened his pace and stepped out onto the terrace, scanning the ocean. No Phoebe.

The property was completely secure; she couldn't be

anywhere else. But knowing that didn't lead him to feel any calmer. He checked the house again and this time, found her. Asleep. No wonder she hadn't responded when he'd called her name. She'd drifted off on a sun lounger on the back deck, mercifully in the shade thrown by a nearby tree. She wore a singlet top and shorts, so her golden legs were on display, crossed at the ankle, and her breasts shifted with each gentle breath.

He stood staring at her, his nostrils flaring, his temperature rising, his hands balling into fists as he remembered what it had been like to make love to her, to know her body as intimately as he'd ever known anyone. He didn't make a sound, and yet she shifted, sighed, pressing her hand to her stomach, then blinking up at him. Her lips shaped into a smile, full and generous and attributable only to the fact she was still half dreaming.

'What time is it?' she asked, groggily, sitting up and looking around.

'Just after three.'

She blinked. 'I've been asleep for hours.'

'Yesterday was a big day.'

She pulled a face. 'Yeah.'

He wondered at the pulling in the centre of his chest, the slightly painful stitching sensation. 'Did you enjoy any of it, Phoebe?'

Her eyes widened. 'It…wasn't about enjoyment. It's something we had to do, right?'

He should have been glad to hear her speak so pragmatically. It was exactly what he wanted his bride to feel—and to understand he felt. But Phoebe deserved more after everything she'd already been through.

'It was an experience I'll never forget,' she elaborated. 'That beautiful tiara—what an honour to have worn it.'

He moved to sit on the edge of the sun lounger. There wasn't much space, so it brought them close together and Phoebe's breath hitched in her throat.

'And the dress was really nice, too. That was amazing how Marie was able to organise it so quickly. I had no idea that could be done. And I loved meeting Xiomara. She's lovely.'

Phoebe was babbling. In a very un-Phoebe manner.

Phoebe was nervous.

Because of him. Nervous good? Nervous bad? Nervous because she couldn't stop thinking about how much she wanted him?

'And the food was great. I loved it. My mum tried to make Castilonian food often, but she never quite got it right. It was—'

'Phoebe,' he interrupted, hearing the surrender in his tone and not caring. 'I want to kiss you.'

Phoebe's lips parted, her concentration visibly wavered, her gaze falling to his mouth. Everything inside of him tightened in anticipation. He'd vowed to wait until she asked, until she begged, but here he was, begging. Needing. Wanting so much it hurt.

He moved forward a little, his body flushed with heat. In the back of his mind, he heard the warning voice. The reminder that the more he wanted someone or something, the smarter it was to back away. It was how he'd lived his life—having had any affection withdrawn from him once his parents died, he'd naturally developed a coping mechanism that had him avoid relying on anyone. Needing anyone.

But sex was different. It was something his body felt and wanted, not his head nor heart. And Phoebe couldn't hurt his body.

Except, hadn't the last month and a half hurt him? Physically, at least? He'd barely slept that first month...

Don't do this.

The wise counsel in his mind should have been obeyed, but Octavio was too far gone to care. It wouldn't last. That was his sole consolation. At some point, the sexual infatuation would burn out, and everything would be normal again.

And it *was* an infatuation, the kind Octavio had never known. But he'd heard about it. He knew it wasn't rare or unusual. It was just a phase between two people who happened to have a certain chemistry.

He paused, close enough to her lips to kiss her, but doing no such thing. Not until she said something. Anything. He'd kissed her before without her issuing a verbal invitation, but this was different. He needed her to admit she wanted him as well. He was out on a limb and didn't want to be the only one. Perhaps he also wanted to demonstrate to himself that he was still in control. He wanted her but he wasn't lost to her.

Phoebe didn't say anything though. Instead, she closed the rest of the distance between them and claimed his mouth with her own, melding them in a way that made him—and her—moan in awareness and completion. It was the kiss he'd wanted to give her on their wedding day, the kiss that should have sealed their marriage ceremony. It was a kiss that lit every part of him on fire, igniting deep in his soul.

Her body was warm from the sun. He felt it as he

pressed himself against her, the sweet roundness of her stomach, her beautiful breasts, he kissed her until she was writhing beneath him and the word *please* was flicking into his mouth like the tail-end of a whip, mesmerising him, calling to him, weakening any thoughts he'd had of restraint, any idea that this could just be a kiss.

It could never be just a kiss with them. That was their chemistry. He moved his body over hers, straddling her and kissing her, running his hands through her hair while he tasted her mouth, then removed her shirt, groaning at the sight of her braless body, her beautiful breasts. He remembered them, but they were different now. Fuller, the nipples a darker pink. He dropped his head to one, hungry to feel it in his mouth, needing to roll her nipple with his tongue and revelling in the way she arched her back and screamed his name when he did so.

This felt good. So bloody good. Control was still his; or if it wasn't, it was something neither of them had.

He ran his hand down to her stomach, pausing because emotions threatened to punch him in the gut and he didn't want to *feel* anything but the physical.

'It's fine.' Phoebe stroked his back. 'I asked the doctor at my last check-up.' He glanced up at her in time to see her cheeks flush pink. 'Just *in case* something like this happened. My pregnancy is low-risk, so far as twin pregnancies go. There's no medical reason for us not to—um—I mean, if that's where this is going.'

Her awkwardness and nervousness pulled at something dangerously close to his heart. He wasn't sure what he would say if he spoke, so he didn't say anything. He just went back to kissing her, longer, slower, more sensually, drawing this out to torment them both. And it was a torment. A torment to be so rock-hard against her sex but to have clothing separating them, a torment to have her naked breasts pressed to his chest through the fabric of his shirt. A torment to kiss her and not be inside of her. But he wanted to make this last, he wanted to maintain control.

Finally, it was too much for Octavio, and he stripped their clothes piece by piece, still making himself take his time, tracing her body with his tongue, flicking her breasts, her stomach, her hips, her sex, before finally he separated her legs.

'Would you prefer me to use a condom?'

She laughed. 'That horse has bolted, hasn't it?'

'I mean from a health point of view. I'm clean, but if you'd prefer me to take the precaution—'

'Oh, gosh, I hadn't even thought—' She shook her head. 'I am, too. I'm not exactly someone who does this often, and I've always used protection in the past. Always.'

He knew that, but for some reason in that moment, in that context, it made him feel powerful. Masculine. Special. He boxed those feelings away. All of them, especially the last one.

He wasn't special. Sure, he was King, but that was not the same thing as mattering to someone, and it had been a long time since he had.

Relief at not having to leave her to go in search of the condoms he had stashed somewhere in the villa was palpable. He positioned himself at her sex, looking down at her, realising he'd never done this with Phoebe. In the past when they'd been together, he'd entered her without looking at her face. Not intentionally, but simply because he'd been caught up in passion and had been at a fever pitch, desperate to lose himself in her. Now, as he pressed into her, he found his eyes were hooked to Phoebe's and wouldn't shift. He saw the way her pupils swelled and irises darkened, the way her skin flushed a darker shade of pink, the way she bit into her lip as if to stop from screaming out. He saw something shift inside of her gaze, something that pummelled him and threatened to break him, so finally he tore his eyes away, burying his head in the crook of her neck as he thrust into her completely and stayed there, buried deep. Her muscles tightened around his length and he was euphoric. It had been way too long and he'd wanted this way too much.

He surrendered completely.

He had lost himself to her, staring at her as she'd climaxed, marvelling at her beauty, her passion, at how alive she was. Marvelling at the fact she was his wife, that she would be the mother of his children. Marvelling at the fact she was his.

And was he hers, too?

He'd shut the thought down, even when he knew the answer. When it came to sex, yes. He was hers. Every inch of him was. She made him feel things he'd never known, and there was no point denying it. But even as his body had given up any pretence of self-protection, his mind refused to.

Sex was sex. That's all this was. He was capable of separating the physical from anything else. Beyond this, they were two people thrown together by circumstance. That was something else they had to navigate, but the fact they'd slept together shouldn't complicate it.

'God, I've missed that,' he said, afterwards, pulling

away from her and stroking the side of her face. She went from sensually languid to confused to…different. Not languid at all.

'Me, too.' But her voice was a little strained. Why?

'You're okay?' Had he hurt her? He'd tried to be gentle but hell, it had been a long time…

'Oh, yes. I'm fine. It's fine.' She smiled, but was he imagining a tightness in her features?

'Are you hungry?'

'Um, yeah. I guess so.'

'Okay. I'll go reheat something.' He pulled away from her with regret, but consoled himself that things were different now. Having done that once, he knew it would happen again. Tonight? 'Take your time.'

She did take her time. She needed to. Something cool had slid into her veins and she needed to regroup, to make sure she didn't show him how she was feeling.

Which was what?

Ambivalent?

Uncertain?

Hurt?

But why?

I missed that. Not, *I missed you.*

It was semantics, she knew that, but it didn't change the fact that he'd yet again made her feel as though sex was all he cared about. He'd missed sleeping with her. That wasn't the same as missing her.

Whereas she'd missed him?

She closed her eyes on a tremulous breath, moving towards the railing and looking out to sea. She'd pulled the same clothes back on, and her shirt was sun warmed from where he'd tossed it on the terrace.

Yes. She had missed him. She'd missed sex with him, too, but she'd missed more than that, and it was a terrifying thing to admit, because it was abundantly clear that Octavio viewed her exactly as Christopher had.

Sex.

Convenient, meaningless sex.

Extra convenient for Octavio, because he now had a queen and a couple of heirs on the way, and he hadn't needed to go through the rigmarole of a long royal engagement. Plus, they were great in bed together, which wasn't necessarily a foregone conclusion with the Princess he'd been intending to marry.

So all of Octavio's boxes were ticked. But what about Phoebe's?

Prior to meeting Octavio, she'd sworn off men. Her experience with Christopher had been more than enough. But once she'd found out she was pregnant, she'd been in a total panic. The thought of being a single mother had terrified her. She'd known she'd cope, but she also knew how difficult it would be, particularly given her lack of education.

'Phoebe?' His voice interrupted her thoughts, and she turned, still frowning contemplatively.

He'd dressed, too, in a pair of navy blue shorts and a crisp white shirt with the sleeves pushed up to his elbows. He looked good enough to eat. She looked away again.

'The food is ready.'

'Okay. Coming.'

And just when she thought she'd mostly got her head around where things stood between them, he reached down and caught her hand and lifted it to his lips, kissing the skin on her upturned palm. Goose bumps spread across her skin, and the ice in her veins began to thaw, just a little.

CHAPTER TEN

'MIND IF I ask you something?'

She looked at him, her mouth full of the saffron-infused rice he'd heated for their lunch, and nodded. They'd chosen to sit at the kitchen table, which was an informal yet beautiful space with views towards the front garden and cove. Phoebe thought she would never grow tired of this view. It was heartwarmingly beautiful. When she'd finished eating, she said, 'You're the King, aren't you? I'm pretty sure you don't have to ask my permission for anything.'

'With you, I'm just Octavio. Just like I said that first night we met.'

Her smile was wistful. Things had seemed so simple then. It had almost felt as though fate had thrown them together for that one night, because it knew he needed a comfort that only she could give and because she'd needed...what? To move on? To officially put an end to the chapter with Christopher by sleeping with someone else? Perhaps that had motivated her in part.

'Phoebe?'

She startled a little. 'Yes. I'm listening.'

He was too perceptive to have missed the fact she'd drifted off into her own thoughts. She focused on him now.

'Why did you choose to work at the *clínica*?'

Her brows knit together. 'What do you mean?'

'You were working as an administrator in a school. There must have been a lot of jobs you could have applied for.'

'Oh.' She nodded. 'Well, the pay was good, for one thing. And I guess…' She sighed a little. 'My mother worked as a cleaner at a hospital. When I saw the listing, I sort of felt… I don't know. It sounds so stupid, but I almost felt as if she was guiding me towards the job. Like maybe she was pulling strings.' Then, aware of how fanciful it sounded, she cleared her throat. 'Plus, the hours were flexible, and the notice period virtually non-existent. I wanted a job I could walk out of if—'

'If?'

'If I found my dad.'

Octavio's expression was sympathetic. 'Tell me what you know of him?'

'Not a lot. His name and the fact that mum was pretty sure he lived in the capital.'

'She didn't tell you anything else about him?'

'Nothing that would help me find him.' She sighed, pushing the paella around her plate. 'She said he loved music, that he played guitar as if taught by angels, that he sang beautifully and could swim like a fish. She told me he was kind and patient but that they both knew their fling would be brief. He left without giving her his number or email address or anything. She didn't even have a photograph.'

Octavio's frown deepened. 'That's it?'

She nodded. 'I've given all this to the investigator I hired.'

'And has the investigator turned up any information?'

'Not yet. I'm hopeful every day though.' She pleated her napkin. 'I know it's like looking for a needle in a haystack but I'd love to know who he is.'

'You have a lot of resources at your command, Phoebe. My security forces can help, you know.'

Her eyes widened. 'I hadn't thought of that.'

'When we get back, I'll arrange a meeting. You can go through everything with them. Maybe the palace will be able to find him.'

'Maybe.' Butterflies ignited in her stomach.

'And then he'll learn not only that he has a daughter, but also that she is Queen of his country.'

'That's a little overwhelming,' she said with a grimace. 'I'm not sure how he'll feel about that.'

'He'll be thrilled to know you, Phoebe. He'll think he's won the lottery.'

'Because I'm Queen?'

He reached out and put his hand on hers. 'Because you're you.'

Phoebe's heart turned over in her chest. She pulled her hand away quickly, rubbing it against her leg beneath the table.

Christopher had been charming, too. Christopher had said things that had made her feel so special and wonderful, as though he was the luckiest man on earth, and it had all been a lie.

'Don't say things like that.'

'Why not?'

'Because it's not…it's not what we are.'

'So I'm not allowed to compliment you?'

She shook her head. 'I don't need it. I don't want it. We barely know one another.'

He frowned at her characterisation but she refused to be swayed.

'If it hadn't been for the baby, we would never have seen one another again.'

'That was your choice, not mine.'

'There was no choice about it. You were offering something I could never have accepted.'

His frown deepened. 'More time with me?'

'As your mistress.' Her nostrils flared. 'Do you have any idea what that felt like?'

'I said *lover*, not *mistress*.'

'It's the same thing. You made it clear I wasn't suitable for anything but secret sex. What kind of woman, with a modicum of self-respect, would accept that?'

'I'm not your ex,' he said quietly. 'It's natural that you would conflate us in your mind, but I am not him. I was not intending to do the wrong thing by you. I was not intending to use you. I certainly didn't intend to lie to you.'

She bit into her lip. All that was true, but he'd still hurt her in the same way Christopher had. She'd still felt betrayed by his request. Offended, angry, hurt, hollowed out. Devalued and cheap.

'I thought that by laying my cards on the table, there would be no room for problems. I wanted to keep seeing you, but not to risk leading you on. Our chemistry is something that would be easy to mistake for…more. I didn't want to risk that in spending time together you might mistake our physical relationship for something like love. It happens, you know?'

She tilted her face away from him, staring out to sea,

suddenly wishing she were far, far away from him and here, that she were out on the ocean, floating on her back in the shape of a star, limbs spread wide. Even there though, she suspected this feeling would follow her. She wasn't sure where she could go that would leave her safe.

'Has it happened to you?' She wasn't really interested, but she felt she needed to say something to buy some time. To enable herself to recover some equilibrium and seem something like normal.

'I'm always careful.'

Always. She turned to face him then, scanning his features. 'It can't have been easy for you to date.'

'No,' he agreed.

'You have lived your whole life in the spotlight.'

He dipped his head in agreement.

'So how did you do it?'

'The same way I did with you.'

Something panged in her chest. None of this was new for him. It was all the same.

'By being honest, ensuring discretion.'

'How did you know you could trust me?' she asked, pressing her chin into her palm, elbow resting on the tabletop.

His lips tugged downwards. 'I don't know.'

'I mean, I was working as a cleaner and selling sordid details of our night together could have earned me a lot of money...'

'I know.'

'So, wasn't that a risk for you to take?'

'I wasn't myself that night.'

'So ordinarily, you wouldn't have approached me?'

The silence stretched between them. She didn't know

why it mattered so much. She was trying to get to grips with her own feelings but delving into his wasn't helping.

'I'd like to say no, but in all sincerity, there was something about you. I'd noticed you, even before I spoke to you.'

Phoebe's heart trembled dangerously. 'What had you noticed about me?'

'Your grace.' For some reason, she loved that he'd said something beyond the mere physical. It wasn't her hair or her eyes, but an expression of who she was. 'You walk as though you are listening to classical music. You walk as though you are dancing in your mind. I find it mesmerising.'

Her stomach swooped.

'I didn't realise.'

'I cannot be the first person to point that out to you?'

A memory hovered on the periphery of her mind. A warm memory, that made her smile. 'My mother actually used to say that, too.'

'Did she?'

Phoebe nodded. 'She enrolled me in a couple of free "come and try" dance classes. I loved it. Ballet, particularly.'

'Did you continue to study?'

'No.'

'Why not?'

'She couldn't afford it. Nor could she get me to class reliably. She often worked two jobs, just to cover our bills.'

Sympathy softened his eyes but Phoebe tilted her chin. 'She was an incredible woman. I will always be proud of her for how hard she worked. She tried her best, every day. And it wasn't easy. She wanted better for me.' Phoebe pressed her palm to her stomach. 'So you can imagine how I felt when I realised I was going to be returning home to walk in her footsteps—a single mother, with a father who may or may not want anything to do with us.' She blinked quickly. 'At least, that's what I thought, when I found out I was pregnant.'

His voice was soft, but rumbly. Deep, as if drawn from the very depths of his chest. 'That would never have been your fate. From the moment I learned of the pregnancy, I have wanted to be here, to support you, to be a father.'

Tears threatened. She blinked again. 'I know that now.'

He expelled a breath and she had the sense he was holding something back, perhaps waiting until later. 'What did she want for you, Phoebe?'

Her mother. Phoebe pressed her fork into the paella thoughtfully. 'Just something better.' She tasted the rice, swallowed, then took a sip of her water. 'But then she got sick, and I had to leave school.'

More sympathy in Octavio's eyes. She focused on a point over his shoulder. His sympathy made her want to cry. Worse, it made her want to stand up and walk around the table, sit in his lap and let him put his arms around her. To hold her until his strength seeped into her and she felt whole again.

She'd been strong for so long. Strong on her own. It had been such a burden to carry, but she couldn't share that with Octavio. She couldn't ask it of him. That's not what they were. His words were burned into her brain, and she knew she'd need to hold them like a talisman in order to keep a cool head in all this.

'What kind of sick?'

'Cancer.' She toyed with her hair, pulling it over one shoulder. 'She only lived a year after her diagnosis. It was very aggressive.' Tears sparkled on Phoebe's lashes then. 'I was devastated.'

'You must have been. What happened to you, Phoebe? You were only seventeen and an orphan. Where did you live?'

She shrugged softly. 'I just didn't tell anybody. I kept paying rent until the lease ended, I kept going through the motions, but meanwhile, I was packing up Mum's stuff and working out what the hell to do with my life. I missed her so much it felt like I'd been shot.' She shook her head. 'I was just in a grief fog, I think.'

He nodded with genuine understanding.

'When did you get the job at the school?'

'That's what I was doing all along,' she clarified. 'When my mum got sick and I needed work. An old teacher of mine had moved there—she got the job for me. It was just basic admin work.'

He reached across then, finding the hand she'd withdrawn from him earlier, and weaving their fingers together, making it harder for her to pull away from him. Not that she wanted to.

'And eventually, you met Christopher.'

Her stomach dropped. She thought of Christopher, his steely blue eyes, dimpled cheeks, short blond hair. She thought of the way she used to look at him and believe him to be the most handsome, perfect man in the world. She thought of all the things she'd thought and how wrong she'd been, and it was a perfect reminder that she couldn't trust her instincts. She couldn't trust that what she felt was actually true. She'd been so wrong about him.

'Yes.'

'Tell me, *querida*, what was the age difference between the two of you?'

Her skin prickled with goose bumps at the easy way he slid the term of endearment into the question. It meant nothing though. He'd used the same phrase the first time they'd been together. It was just habit for Octavio, it didn't mean anything. None of this did.

Reluctance held her silent a moment. 'He was older.'

'How much older?'

She bit into her lip. 'About ten years.'

Octavio's eyes darkened. 'And did he know about your mother?'

'Yes,' she said quietly. 'One of the teachers said something. He'd remarked on me being very quiet, so she'd told him why.'

'I see.'

'What do you see?'

'A man who recognised a vulnerable, grieving young woman and turned that to his advantage.'

'The same could be said of you and me,' she pointed out. Then quickly added, lest he misunderstand her comparison, 'You were grieving. Did I take advantage of you?'

'We both know the opposite is true.'

'Oh, really? How did you take advantage of me?'

His thumb stroked the flesh on the back of her hand. 'Perhaps you were intimidated by me? I am the King. Maybe you felt you had to say yes to me?'

She gasped. 'Don't. Don't say that. Don't turn—what that night was—into that.'

He scanned her face. 'What was that night?'

Heat flushed through her. She felt dangerously close to a precipice she didn't even want to approach, let alone tip over. 'It was *not* that. I didn't care that you're a king. I never did. You asked me to call you Octavio and I did. You were…a man. And I was a woman. And what we shared that night had nothing to do with your position or power or pressure. It was about us wanting each other, wanting to comfort each other. It was a moment of shared madness, sure, but it wasn't a case of anyone being taken advantage of. You can't really think that?'

'No,' he admitted after a beat, and he smiled in a way that made her feel as though she were floating. 'But I'm relieved to hear you don't either.'

She squeezed his hand as a prelude to pulling away, but he held tight and she gave up quickly. It was a weakness, but she liked the way it felt to be intertwined like this.

'It's incredible to think that our babies were conceived that night, and we had no idea.'

'I used protection,' he said, rubbing his spare hand over his jaw.

'I know.'

'You're not on the pill?'

She shook her head. 'Christopher and I had discussed trying for a baby as soon as we were married.' Her voice cracked a little. She'd never get over how duplicitous he'd been, and how completely she'd fallen for his lies.

Octavio's eyes narrowed. 'When were you to marry?'

'About a month after I found out about his wife.'

He swore. 'That seems like a very lucky escape.'

'Yes.'

She looked away quickly. 'We were going to elope. Just the two of us. We were going to go to the South Island, choose somewhere remote and pristine and say our vows, just the two of us. I thought that was so romantic, but now I get it. He just wanted to make sure no one from his real world saw us. I have no idea how he was going to pull it off—I guess a fake minister to conduct the ceremony or something?' She shook her head, anger firing through her now where hurt and grief had once been. 'I can't believe I didn't see through it.'

'Being trusting is not a character flaw.'

'Yes, it is. I was trusting to a fault, and that's not a mistake I'll ever make again.'

'You can trust me,' he said, quietly, with intensity, squeezing her hand as if to reinforce that.

'No, I can't.' She pulled her hand away properly now, reinforcing the fact she was on her own. 'I know you're nothing like him, but I can't trust you; I can't trust *anyone*.' She sighed again. 'The thing is, I guess when it boils down to it, I don't trust myself. I went out with Christopher for years and was so in love with him I just didn't question anything.'

Octavio's features tightened visibly. 'His levels of deception were incredible.'

'But I didn't realise. I didn't suspect. I don't trust my instincts any more. I don't trust my perceptions of people.'

'Okay,' he conceded, rather than pushing a point she was stuck on. 'But let me say this—I will never lie to you. If I say something, it's the truth. That's who I am.'

She nodded, because she knew it was the only way to end the conversation. And she knew that he was probably being sincere. Phoebe also knew that regardless of his assurance, she would continue to protect herself by doubting, by believing him—and everyone—to be capable of the worst. If she'd done that with Christopher, she'd never have been hurt.

'He contacted me the other day, you know,' she volunteered spontaneously.

Octavio's whole bearing changed.

'Christopher?' His voice was sharp. Phoebe glanced at him, nodding once.

Octavio swore. 'He called you?'

'No, he sent a message through the app we used to use.'

'Did you reply?'

She shook her head. 'No. Why?'

'You can't speak to him.'

Phoebe narrowed her eyes. She hadn't been planning to, but the way he was telling her what to do rankled. 'It's really not any of your business.'

'I beg your pardon, but you are my wife.'

A shiver ran down her spine. Not a bad shiver, but a delicious, delightful shiver of warmth. Despite everything she'd just said, despite everything she knew to be true in her heart, hearing him call her his wife so possessively, so intently, set a fire in her bloodstream.

'I am also my own person.'

'Not any more you're not. You are Queen of Castilona and you are a target. People will be trying to sell stories about you for the rest of your life. This man cannot be trusted, Phoebe. If you engage with him again, he will betray you.'

Anger and something like crushing disappointment mingled in her belly, making her throat feel acidic. 'I know that,' she hissed, scraping back her chair and standing. 'He's ruined my life once already. Do you think I'd give him a chance to do it again?'

Octavio stared at her though, a muscle ticking in the base of his jaw. 'It wasn't that long ago that you broke up. Do you still love him?'

'I hate him.'

'You can love someone and hate them at the same time.'

She pulled a face. 'No.' She was emphatic. 'I don't love him. He's nothing to me.'

'Then it should be easy to ignore his message.'

'Which is what I was planning to do. You don't need to tell me how to act, Octavio. I'm not stupid.'

'Except with him—'

'Don't say it.' She held up a hand, silencing the rest of that sentence. 'I already think the worst of myself for how I was with Christopher. I don't need you to reinforce that.'

He glared at her, the angry words they'd exchanged sparking in the air around them. Octavio controlled his temper first.

'I meant to protect you, not to undermine you. I know you understand what you should do, but when it comes to relationships, things get murkier.'

'I never want to see nor speak to him again.'

'Okay.' Octavio nodded slowly, but it was clear to Phoebe he didn't completely believe her. Maybe he'd learned the lesson she'd been preaching: trust no one. It was just safer that way.

Octavio watched her walk away, a sinking feeling taking over his body. He didn't like it.

He didn't like the way that conversation—argument—had made him feel. He didn't like anything about it. He didn't like her revelations about her ex, what the other man had done to Phoebe, how he'd lied to her and treated her. He didn't like to think how close she'd come to marrying the guy, how eager she'd been to have his baby. He didn't like to think that in an alternate reality, in which Phoebe hadn't discovered the truth, she *would* be married to him by now, perhaps still blissfully unaware of Christopher's duplicity.

But most of all, Octavio hadn't liked the way it had felt to learn that the other man still had a way of reaching out to Phoebe, of contacting her. Of trying to reignite their relationship?

Phoebe surely wouldn't be so stupid, after what he'd done, but the fact there'd been contact between them had flooded his body with ice and something else. Something foreign and unwelcome.

Anger.

The kind of anger Octavio had learned to steer well clear of, because it was counterproductive and clouded one's judgement. Courtesy of his uncle's cruelty, most of Octavio's life had been an exercise in control and restraint.

Only he hadn't felt restrained tonight.

He hadn't felt in control. He'd listened to Phoebe and had felt a violent rage towards Christopher. And then, when he'd learned about the text, he'd felt something else. Something that veered a lot towards jealousy.

He scraped his chair back, as if he could physically reject that feeling. *Jealousy?*

Impossible.

That's not what he and Phoebe were. So she had a past? Big deal. He was her present and her future, and in many ways, their relationship was exactly what he'd needed. She was providing him with the heirs he badly needed, but more than that, their chemistry was like a drug. He just had to be careful not to get hooked. And not to get confused. She was his wife, his lover, the future mother of his children, but they were not a couple, and that was just how Octavio intended for things to remain.

CHAPTER ELEVEN

THEY SLEPT IN the same bed and they made love as if it was the last chance they had to be together—with desperate, fervent passion—but in the morning, a sense of restraint was still between them. A tension that tugged at Phoebe and frustrated her. She didn't want to fight with Octavio. She didn't want to be here in this beautiful, beachside paradise and be at odds with the man she'd married. The man she was having twins with.

And so, as he pulled a fruit platter from the fridge and placed it on the counter, Phoebe took a seat on the stool opposite and rested her chin on her palm, doing everything she could to appear nonchalant even when her tummy was in knots.

'Tell me about your cousin Xiomara,' she started, her voice a little tremulous.

He glanced at her, offering a smile. A tight smile, but at least it was an attempt at civility. Her gut churned. Why should she care if he was annoyed at her? But why *would* he be annoyed at her? Because of their argument yesterday? Or because Christopher had messaged her? She wasn't in control of the latter, or even the former, when it came to it.

'What would you like to know?'

'I like her,' Phoebe said with a lift of her shoulder. 'She was so kind to me on our wedding day. She didn't have to be, but she really took me under her wing.'

'That's Xiomara.' He flicked on the coffee machine and slipped a mug beneath it. The kitchen filled with the aroma of caffeine as it whirred to life.

'You're friends with her?'

He hesitated almost imperceptibly, but Phoebe caught it. 'Yes.'

'Her father is Mauricio,' Phoebe prompted.

Octavio's eyes lifted to Phoebe's. 'Nobody's perfect.'

The joke tugged at Phoebe's lips, drawing a smile from her, and she felt the cracking of their tension, the easing of awkwardness with that one simple quip.

She breathed out.

'You don't like him.'

Octavio looked at her with a hint of bemusement. 'That's well established.'

'Why not?'

Octavio slid a coffee across to Phoebe, then set about making himself one. She lifted the drink to her nose and inhaled it. The doctor had assured her coffee—in strict moderation—was fine, and while she'd been happy to give up almost anything for the babies, this cup of half-strength coffee in the morning was one of life's greatest pleasures.

One of.

Her eyes lifted to Octavio reflexively, as her mind replayed the way they'd spent the small hours of the morning, and she flushed to the roots of her hair. 'Thank you,' she murmured.

His gaze was slightly teasing as it fixed on her, as though he'd read her thoughts.

She lifted the cup to her lips partly to conceal her face from him.

'My uncle is...' He hesitated, frowning, turning away to make his own coffee, so she realised he was doing his share of face hiding as well. 'He's nothing like my father,' Octavio said after a pause.

'Your father was oldest?' she asked, then realised how silly that question was, because of course Octavio's father, who'd been King before Octavio, had been the oldest. 'Never mind. Dumb question.'

'Not so dumb, actually,' Octavio said. 'My father was older, yes, but by only a few minutes.'

'They were twins,' she said on an exhalation, something prickling her spine—a sense of history repeating itself. She pressed a hand to her own stomach, as if she could communicate with the babies there.

Octavio nodded, turning back to face her, coffee cup clasped in one strong, tanned hand. 'All his life, Mauricio resented my father for something which he could not control. My father had been born first. By the law of the land, he was therefore the heir to the throne.'

She winced. 'That must have been hard, for everyone.'

'Yes and no. My father didn't have a resentful bone in his body. He was naturally very good at things. Sport, academics, he was well-liked, popular. Power came easy to him. Even without his title, his command was apparent.'

'Sounds like someone else I know,' she said, with sincerity.

Octavio's smile was automatic, almost dismissive. She wondered if he recognised the truth of her words.

'I think generally, twins are quite close. Almost code-pendent. The same could not be said for my father and Mauricio. For every accomplishment my father enjoyed, Mauricio seemed to act as though he was being robbed.'

'How do you know this?'

Octavio rubbed a hand over his jaw. 'Things I heard as a boy, things I've learned since, things I've read—quotes that Mauricio stupidly gave to journalists when he was in a fit of pique.'

'Why then would your parents nominate him to serve as your Regent?'

'They had no choice. It's enshrined in the constitution.'

'Right, I think I was taught that.'

Her mind had become hazy with all the lessons she'd consumed between getting engaged to Octavio and marrying him. 'Just the essentials,' her tutors had assured her. It hadn't felt at all essential to Phoebe to learn the obscure laws of Castilona, at least not in order to get married, but she'd sat there and paid attention. Mostly.

'Obviously they had no thought of dying. They were young, both in excellent health. Their deaths couldn't have been foreseen.'

'It was a car accident, wasn't it?'

He nodded, but slowly, like he was buried in deep thought. 'They were overseas, for work. Their trip took them to a remote village high on a mountain, where they intended to tour a school. Rain had been forecast, but it turned into a flash flood. Their car was caught in a deluge and pushed off the edge of the cliff.'

She shuddered. It was awful. Truly awful. 'Octavio.' She reached across for his hand, tears sparkling on her lashes. Pregnancy hormones regularly pulled at her emotions, but this was more than that.

'I know,' he said, and something morphed in her body—a sense that they understood one another's deepest thoughts and needs without words. It was a closeness she'd never felt before. But how ridiculous, a voice in her head chastised. They were *not* close. Not in any way but the physical. They were virtual strangers, still dancing around, getting to know one another gradually. Weren't they?

She'd *known* Christopher. Known him for years, but never really understood him. She'd thought she could trust him with her life, and he'd betrayed her. Knowing someone was a fallacy.

She couldn't wrestle with the conundrum a moment longer because Octavio was talking again, almost as if the floodgates had been opened and he couldn't—or didn't want to—close them.

'I remember the day I heard so clearly. Everything about it is burned into my memory. Where I was, the light, the sound of Rodrigo's voice, when he came to tell me. He had been crying—which was unusual for him. He tried to hide it from me, but I could tell by the way his eyes were puffy and his voice raw. He sat me on his lap and held me close and explained to me that my parents were gone but that they would always love me. He told me that not only would my mother and I always have the stars, but she was now amongst them, so all I had to do was look up and see them sparkle and know that she was thinking of me.' He grimaced. 'I was nine—he was doing his best to be age-appropriate.'

'It sounds like he did a good job to me.' She dashed at her eyes, forestalling the tears that were threatening.

'From then, it was a whirlwind of change. Mauricio was quickly announced as Regent, ruling in my name until my twenty-eighth birthday.'

'Why so old? Why not eighteen or twenty-one, or even twenty-five?'

'Tradition. A tradition that had not, until me, been tested. It was an arbitrary number, decided upon several generations ago. I'm the first monarch to have been held powerless until that age because of the law.'

She sipped her coffee, a hand on her stomach on autopilot. 'You don't feel Mauricio did a good job?'

'I know he didn't,' Octavio said, his voice like steel. 'Everything Mauricio did was about consolidating his own power. I am still not convinced that he wasn't moving the pieces into place to stage a coup, closer to my coronation.'

She gasped.

'He installed loyal friends into the highest military positions, promoted his allies into important political roles. It will take years to gradually weed out troublemakers and ensure our government is working for the good of the people. For his entire regency, his focus was on how he might retain power, even after he was removed.'

'And has he?'

His eyes glittered. 'To some extent, yes.'

She blinked.

'It is one of the reasons I insisted on us sharing my apartment, in the palace.'

'Because the staff might leak to him?'

He hesitated a little. 'And because I needed to know

you would be safe.' There was an uneasiness to his voice. Her heart fizzed and popped in her chest. His concern for her was like a firework, but she quickly understood it was not *her* he was worried about, but the babies she carried. That thought was confirmed a moment later when he added, 'Our children are a threat to him. If he could depose me, then he would be King. Once these babies are born...'

'You can't seriously think he means to fight you for the throne? Or that he would do anything to hurt our twins?'

His features, for a moment, seemed to tighten with sheer exhaustion. 'My parents were killed in an accident,' he said slowly, eyes raking her face, as if trying to understand something. 'But before they set off on that road trip, a report was issued from the village to the palace that flash flooding was expected. The report never made it to my parents' driver, nor their security detail.'

Phoebe gasped again, pressing her palm against her mouth. 'You think Mauricio did that?'

'I suspect, yes. It would be impossible to prove now. He's had too long to cover his tracks. But he was at the palace, and even then, he was currying favour in the hopes of gaining power in his own right.'

She bit into her lip. 'Oh, Octavio. I can't believe anyone would be so cruel.'

'Rodrigo suspected it. He was asking questions. And so, Mauricio had him exiled.'

She squeezed her eyes shut. It was damning, if circumstantial, evidence.

'He shut out his own brother, cut him off financially and, as it happened, effectively killed him. I appreciate it might seem far-fetched, but do you understand why I would not take risks with you?'

She nodded slowly.

'And why we had to marry quickly? Even a week seemed too long to wait, when I imagined what strings Mauricio might be pulling.'

'But you invited him to the wedding—'

'To not have done so would have drawn the kind of speculation I prefer to avoid. My intention is to remove Mauricio's thumbprints, his stranglehold, from the country, from government, and then I shall decide how to deal with him.'

Phoebe shivered. Octavio sounded so resolute, it was easy to believe he could achieve anything he wished.

'Won't that cause problems for you with Xiomara?'

He studied Phoebe a long while. 'I hope not.'

'But if it does?'

'I have to do what's right.' There was an uneasiness in the admission, and she felt the weight he carried, all on those broad shoulders of his. She stared at him and his eyes locked to hers, the air around them charging with voltage, so she struggled to look away, even as her cells were dancing with little electric shocks.

'Do you trust Xiomara?' she asked, trying to focus on their conversation.

'With my life.'

'Why, when she's his daughter?'

'She is nothing like him,' he said, as though it were so simple. 'Xiomara is loyal. She doesn't speak badly about him, but even as children, when Mauricio would delight in punishing me for no reason, by taking away things of value to me, she would sneak into my room with a treat and sit with me until I felt better.'

Indignation fired her blood. 'He did *what*?' Her voice was halfway to a screech.

Octavio shook his head. 'It was a long time ago.'

'So not only did he rule in your name, he was your legal guardian?'

'Only once Rodrigo was exiled,' Octavio said darkly. 'My parents had no control over who could rule the country in my name, but they did have a say over my guardianship. Rodrigo was appointed shortly after my birth.'

'And so that bastard sent him away.' She shook her head.

'With Rodrigo gone, every parental decision fell to Mauricio. He must have hated me, *querida*. For who I was, what I was destined to become, and most of all because I am so like my father.'

She blanched. 'He should have *loved* you for all those reasons.'

'Hatred is all he is capable of feeling.'

'That's his loss,' she said angrily. 'I don't know how I'll ever be able to be in the same room as this beast of a man again without giving him a piece of my mind.'

Octavio's laugh surprised her. Deep and throaty, it set fires in her pulse when she least expected it. 'While I appreciate the sentiment, I don't need you to protect me. I am more than capable of looking after myself.'

She stared at him and acknowledged that he was right. Octavio could look after himself, easily, *now*. He was smart and strong and powerful, and commanded as most men breathed. But what about the boy he'd been? What about the dear little nine-year-old who'd been shockingly orphaned and was cast adrift from the parents he'd loved, and then the uncle he was closest to, to be raised by a man who saw the throne as his stolen birthright?

'Yes, well, nonetheless, perhaps you might wish to keep Mauricio and me apart for a while. At least until the maelstrom of my pregnancy hormones has settled.'

He hadn't intended to confide any of that to Phoebe. Much of it was intensely private, thoughts he'd never shared with another soul. But as they'd spoken, and her big, intelligent eyes had stared back at him, her lovely face so expressive, he'd found the words drawn out of him, almost as if they were being magnetically tugged. And he didn't mind.

More than that, he realised she had a right—and a need—to know what he did.

Octavio had immediately installed his security chiefs to manage his own operations—men and women he knew he could trust implicitly. He knew because he'd been recruiting them for two years, silently, stealthily searching for the best of the best. Ex-military with the kind of code of honour that meant they would always turn to Octavio for leadership and would give their lives to protect the throne. He was not immediately worried about his personal safety, nor Phoebe's, so long as she was with him. But he worried about the palace and the deep tendrils Mauricio had been able to plant there, during his long reign. As much as possible, he'd ensured the staff waiting on Phoebe were newly hired by himself, but that wasn't always doable.

Mauricio had been a terrible legal guardian, except

in one way. He had demonstrated to Octavio time and time again how futile it was to let feelings take control.

Mauricio had been cold when compassion had been required. Mauricio had been brutal in how he'd delighted in robbing Octavio of comfort and familiarity, in unsettling his life just as soon as he'd got comfortable. Mauricio held the puppet strings and he'd wanted Octavio to know it.

Octavio would never be like him, except for the fact he had learned to view things through a dispassionate lens. He could zoom out from almost any situation and see the facts calmly, make decisions with ice-cold certainty.

So he had laid out his plans for the marriage to Phoebe, knowing that was how it had to be. And if she wouldn't marry him, he would have kept their babies with him just to protect the children, because without that, the babies would always have been at risk.

And he'd told her the truth for the same reason now: to protect her. Knowing what she was up against and why trusting him was a necessity was the best thing for her and their baby.

He'd told her things he'd never told another soul—but not because he'd wanted to share with Phoebe, per se. This wasn't about them. It was about dispassionately acting in her best interests; it meant nothing.

CHAPTER TWELVE

BEING DRIVEN BACK to the palace was strange. They'd come here after the wedding and Phoebe had felt so estranged from Octavio. But after two nights in close confines, sharing a bed, making love, expressing their deepest thoughts and feelings, Phoebe felt a closeness to Octavio that the palace could very well threaten. Though they sat on opposite sides of the sumptuous back seat of the car, separated by the middle section, his presence seemed to wrap around her, making her skin flush and her heart race.

'You're quiet,' he murmured, as the car cut through the beautiful countryside, the city in the distance reminding her of the real world awaiting them.

'Am I?'

He bumped her knee with his. 'You know you are. Is everything okay?'

His concern warmed her further. 'Yeah,' she agreed. But she glanced at him and his sceptical expression made her smile. 'Okay, I'm not.'

'What is the matter?'

'I'm wondering about what happens next?'

'In what context?'

'When we go back to the palace.' She pulled at a piece

of invisible lint on her trousers. It was an elegant suit, delivered with the rest of the clothes Marie had arranged for Phoebe. She wasn't sure who had packed the bag for her honeymoon, but they'd chosen a selection Phoebe had found beautiful and flattering all at once.

'I'm still not understanding…'

Her cheeks flushed. 'With—this.' She gestured from her chest to his.

'Our marriage?'

'You're really going to make me spell this out, aren't you?' she muttered, glancing towards the driver, who was separated from them by a thick glass screen.

'It's soundproof. Unless you press that button, our conversation remains private.'

She bit into her lip. 'I just mean, we shared a bedroom back there. But in the palace…'

Octavio's eyes darkened. 'It was your decision not to share a bed at the palace before. On our honeymoon, it was your decision to change that. And when we get back, it will still be your decision.'

It was an answer that wasn't an answer, and it didn't tell her what he wanted. She looked towards the side window, watching as the countryside zipped past in a blur of brightly coloured fields and then shocks of green— the vines lush and overgrown as the summer sun did its work to fatten and sweeten the grapes this country was famous for—and in her stomach she felt a tightening knot of frustration.

She'd come to Castilona in a knee-jerk reaction to Christopher's betrayal. She'd come here because she'd always wondered about this place, because she'd felt alone and adrift. She'd come here seeking family and connection, wanting to learn about her father and to understand a part of who she was.

Instead, she'd met Octavio. There were times when they were together that made her feel as though none of that mattered. Nothing mattered that had come before—there was only them, a moment, a shared consciousness, almost. But then reality intruded, and she was reminded of all the reasons this would remain a carefully navigated partnership rather than a true relationship. The fact they were sleeping together couldn't be allowed to derail the fact that neither of them wanted the complications of anything more serious.

'If we were to share a room,' she said, turning back to face him, 'it wouldn't change anything, would it?'

The relief in his face was palpable. He reached across and took her hand. 'No. It couldn't.'

She felt something strong and sharp inside of her. She wanted to believe it was a sense of relief, but it didn't feel or taste like it. This was a bitter sensation, spreading through her and leaving emptiness in its wake.

But she was the one who wanted to be sure they were taking care. Sleeping with him didn't mean she trusted him; it didn't mean she would ever let her guard down with him. How could she, after what Christopher had done to her?

'Well, we can't really have the King sleeping on the sofa for the rest of his life,' she pointed out, as though it were simply a matter of logistics.

'There are other apartments we can move to. Bigger, with extra bedrooms...'

'We're going to need extra bedrooms,' she reminded him, gesturing to her stomach.

'A few extra,' he agreed.

Her insides felt all squishy. She might never risk her heart again, at least not in the romantic sense, but she would fiercely love and protect their children and give them absolutely everything in life. She would no longer be alone. She would no longer feel adrift.

'Yes, a few,' she agreed.

'But not one for me?'

Her eyes locked to his. It felt like an important question, as though it required an important, thought-out answer, but in the end, it was simple. She shook her head, because there was not a single doubt in her mind that when it came to their marriage, the physical side of it was something she couldn't—and didn't want to—fight.

Octavio felt as though he could run ten marathons. He felt as though he could box with a wild bear and win. He felt as though he was a king not just of Castilona but of everyone everywhere. Power thrummed through his veins as he stared down at his wife's passion-ravaged face, her eyes huge, her cheeks flushed, and he had a primal, animalistic thrill because *he* had done that. He had caused her voice to grow hoarse from screaming his name, had caused her to run her nails down his back as though wanting to draw blood and reclaim her sanity.

And when his own pleasure had burst through him, it had been like a wildfire, totally untamed, all-encompassing, dangerously addictive.

Danger?

He pushed the word aside. There was no danger here.

Phoebe was his wife. She was his country's queen, the mother of the children they were expecting. She was his lover. She was many things to him, but none of them represented danger. Each aspect was separate, easily contained, kept distinct from the other, and he would never allow the lines to blur. It was the key to a successful marriage, he was sure of it.

He pulled away from her with regret, but only for a moment. He fell onto his back, the sheets crisp beneath him, and then drew her to his chest, enjoying the feeling of her soft skin against his, her breathing as she exhaled, her breasts crushed to his side. Even her stomach was sensual, growing with the lives he'd put there. Something like euphoria burst through him. It had been a long time since Octavio had felt that everything in his life was going to work out, but with Phoebe at his side and the babies she was growing in his future, he felt a level of complacency he hadn't known in a long time.

Since his parents had died and Rodrigo had been banished.

Since Mauricio had taken over his life.

He stroked her spine slowly, gently, wondering if she would fall asleep? It was late, but he wasn't tired. In fact, he was the opposite—energised after the return from their honeymoon and this—their first night in the palace as a married couple.

It had gone so well.

A shared dinner, during which she'd asked questions about Castilona and its history, the palace and its importance, his goals for the country's future. Her eyes had zipped with excitement, so he'd felt her shared love for this place, despite the fact she'd only been here a matter of months.

What did that matter?

Castilonian blood ran through her veins and that side of her was just waking up, stirring to life. She was Queen of a country to which she belonged but had never known—Octavio could certainly help fix the latter. They agreed that dinner would be a time to strengthen her understanding of Castilona. Though she had tutors, their lessons covered the basics in an academic sense, whereas Octavio spoke with passion and duty, with the loyalty and love of a man raised to rule.

Phoebe had seemed completely swept up in his stories, and he'd enjoyed that feeling, too.

Afterwards, she'd stood and held her hand out to him, inviting him with that simple gesture, but also with her eyes, which seemed almost to plead with him...and he'd pleaded right back, until they were riding a wave of ecstatic contentment together, bodies entwined, pleasure wrapping around them, through them, in a way they both needed.

'Octavio.' She tilted her face, so he felt her eyes on his features. His breathing was still rough, his chest moving with each inhalation. 'May I ask you something personal?'

He continued to stroke her back, ignoring the flicker of wariness in the pit of his gut. Why shouldn't she ask him whatever she wanted? They were married, he'd already shared things with Phoebe that he hadn't intended to and the world hadn't stopped spinning.

'Of course,' he said, his voice easy, hiding his initial reaction to her entreaty.

'After your uncle sent Rodrigo away, where did you live?'

It was the last thing he'd been expecting, and yet it

shouldn't have surprised him. He'd glossed over his childhood, and yet someone as astute as Phoebe must have wondered.

Nonetheless, he tried to keep emotion out of his voice. 'I was moved to a smaller palace, in the south.'

'Why?'

His smile was a ghost of that expression, laced with the kind of bitterness even time couldn't dull. 'He said it was to shield me from the press, from my grief. But in removing me from this palace, he removed me from everything that was familiar, everything that reminded me of my parents. And he surrounded me with new people. New staff, new tutors. A nanny he'd hired.' The final sentence he spoke with undisguised resentment.

'You didn't like her?'

He tried to quell his feelings. To push them deep, deep down, just as he always did. He tried to contain the anger he felt when he reflected on that time in his life, remembered how vulnerable he'd been, how much he'd needed the adults responsible for him to do better. But it was there, whipping through him, like the building of a storm. 'No, *querida*. I didn't like her. I hated her.'

She stroked his chest, her fingers drawing invisible figures of eight. 'Because she wasn't your mother?'

'Because she was awful,' he corrected.

Her fingers stalled a little. 'Actually awful, or awful in a way that you would have felt about anyone who was charged with your care at that time.'

'Her name was Benita,' he said, slowly, and even now, so many years later, a shudder ran through him. 'And when I misbehaved, which according to her was very often, she would lock me in a room no bigger than a wardrobe, with no light except for the tiny sliver that came under the door.'

Phoebe gasped. Her fingers pressed flat, so her palm was against his chest, as if she could reach through time and draw him out of that dark space.

'She said young princes needed to learn to be tough. That she was hard on me for my own good. When I cried—and remember, I was nine, and my parents had just died—she smacked me until I stopped.'

Another gasp, this time more of a half-sob. 'How dare she?' Phoebe pushed up onto her elbow so she could see him better, keeping her body pressed to his side, and he was glad for the physical comfort of her nearness.

'One day, a servant saw her smack me and reported it to palace security. Enough people had been made aware that she was removed. Someone else was sent.'

'Someone better?' she asked hopefully, but with a frown around her eyes that showed she was beginning to understand.

'Someone who didn't use physical violence to punish me,' he said, holding her gaze for a moment and then looking away. 'Marta was the second nanny—'

'The second of how many?' she asked indignantly.

'There were many. I stopped learning their names as I grew older.'

She closed her eyes, her delicate features showing pain and outrage. 'What was Marta like?'

'She also believed I had to be tough. I suppose Mauricio explained this to each of them, because no matter which nanny I mention, they all shared a common trait of cruelty, which was supposed to be for my ultimate benefit.'

Phoebe's eyes sparkled with tears. He felt her indignation. She stroked his side again, her fingers shaking a little.

'Marta would promise things and then withhold them for no reason. A phone call with Rodrigo that was then taken away because I'd made spelling errors, or the promise of a run after dinner that was removed because I'd slept late. Within a few months, I realised that the more I wanted something, the more she delighted in denying it to me. I learned a lot from her, and I don't mean in the academic sense.'

A tear slid down Phoebe's cheek. 'And after Marta?'

'Marta I had for several years. She retired and then there was Ines. She employed a combination of techniques to toughen me up, notably taking me into the bush surrounding my palace and leaving me there, telling me to find my own way home.'

Phoebe gasped. 'You were a *prince*,' she pointed out. 'How dare she? What if something had happened to you?'

'Mauricio would have been delighted.'

Phoebe ground her teeth. 'Did you ever see him?'

'Twice a year I would come back to this palace.'

'He must have wanted to see you a little, then?'

'On the contrary, it was written into my parents' wills.'

Her cheeks flushed with anger. 'Do you think they knew what he would be like?'

'No. I don't think they could have imagined what a cruel and power-hungry man he was. They pitied him, I believe, for his resentment. It made him so small and bitter, and they were both far too kind to be able to understand the things he was capable of.'

'What was it like when you came here?'

'More of the same. I was assigned to a room far away from where I had once lived, far away from all the rooms that were familiar to me. Mauricio delighted in telling me things about my parents that I know to be false. He would hint that both my father and mother had cheated, that they'd never been one hundred per cent sure I wasn't a bastard, that he couldn't see any of my father in me. This, at least, is provably false.'

'You look so like him,' Phoebe murmured, scanning his eyes.

'Yes, and not only that, I have done a DNA test. I didn't trust Mauricio not to go to the papers with the story. If he did, I wanted to have a counter-argument ready to go.'

Another tear rolled down Phoebe's cheek. He wiped it with the pad of his thumb.

'The only good thing about being in the palace was Xiomara.'

Phoebe placed her chin on his chest, eyes still locked to his face.

'She was here, and she would come to find me, work out how to sneak me away from my nanny. We would run and play and she would bring me food from the kitchen—treats, like I'd enjoyed when my parents were alive. With her, the sun started to shine again. I always paid for it, afterwards, but it was worth it.'

'Did she get in trouble?'

'She had her mother to protect her. While her father ruled the kingdom in my name, and also my life for a time, in their family, Mira—my aunt—was in charge, at least of Xiomara. And for Mira, Xiomara could do no wrong,' he added with an affectionate smile.

'Then what about you? Surely Mira could have intervened on your behalf? Surely Xiomara told her how miserable you were?'

'I don't know if she ever understood the extent of it. My nannies did an excellent job of teaching me to be tough, to rely on no one. To trust no one. Besides, my time with Xiomara was too precious to ruin with complaints.' He sighed. 'Also, she was the one person who still treated me like she had before the accident. She'd always looked up to me, seen me as the strong, older cousin. I didn't want that to change by breaking down to her.'

'Oh, Octavio,' she sighed, dropping a kiss to his chest. 'How absolutely awful.'

'Yes. It was. But it's all ancient history now. I am King, and Mauricio will have to live with that.'

She pressed another kiss to his chest; he felt a tear splash down beside where she'd placed her sweet, full lips. 'Despite all his efforts, you are a good man, Octavio. He must hate that.'

'He hates everything about me.'

'Then that's his mistake, and it's his loss.' She looked up at him, and he saw now her cheeks were completely wet with tears.

That was the last thing he'd wanted. He used both palms to wipe them dry.

'Please, don't cry, Phoebe. This is all in the past—none of it matters any more.'

Her smile was twisty, a haunted reflection as she studied him intently. 'Doesn't it?'

Her words haunted him as he fell into a sleep that was fractured by memories of an upbringing he wished to forget.

CHAPTER THIRTEEN

'THIS IS ALL in the past—none of it matters any more.'

Phoebe replayed those words through her mind over and over again in the days that followed. Days that turned into nights and bled into days, which all took on a predictable, comfortable pattern. Days separated from Octavio—often he was gone by the time she woke up, but that was fine, she'd come to expect it. Even when she craved him and wanted to see him, she refused to feel disappointed, because this was the schedule they'd tacitly agreed to stick to.

Besides, in the evenings, she received her compensation. They shared dinner each night, and then they shared a bed, and it was in bed that she felt as though pieces of her were slotting into place—pieces she hadn't even realised were missing. It was there that she felt as though all their barriers slipped away and they were just two people communicating in the most basic and essential way. Neither sought to protect themselves, they were both totally open to and subjugated by the passion they shared. It commanded and controlled them; it *was* them.

It was in bed, a week after their troubling conversation on the matter of his upbringing, that Phoebe lay with her head pressed against Octavio's chest, listening to his heart, and she felt her own heart beating in perfect unison. As though they had been designed to run at the same time, to the same beat. As though they had their own beat, and her heart had somehow managed to find his.

It was a thought that came totally out of nowhere and almost took her breath away with how fully formed and strong it was. But also, how *wrong* it was.

There was no such thing as a silent matching of hearts. How fanciful.

Besides, her heart had nothing to do with Octavio and their marriage. Her heart had nothing to do with anything—Christopher had made sure of that.

But the next night, curled around him, naked and covered in a slight sheen from their lovemaking, her body stretching with the new life they'd created, she felt it again. This time, a physical tug in the region of her heart, as though her body were trying to force her to reach out and grab him. Not just grab him, but to take his broken heart in her own and make it better.

She fell asleep with a small frown on her lips and the undeniable sense that things were morphing beyond her control, in a way she was entirely uncomfortable with.

And then, she had the dream.

The dream that had perhaps been forming on the periphery of her mind for some time. A dream that was born of all the experiences she'd had recently. Her feelings on becoming a mother, her missing her own mother, Octavio's admissions about his treatment at the hands of his uncle.

'All I want is for him to be loved,' a woman's voice whispered through her mind.

Phoebe was standing beyond the palace, looking

through a locked glass window at Octavio. He sat in a chair in the middle of an empty room, staring straight ahead, not seeing her. Phoebe went to knock on the glass, but her hand couldn't quite reach it.

'As a mother, it's what you want most for your child, Phoebe. To know that someone sees them as they are and loves them for that person—flaws, dreams, ambitions, all of it. My Tavi deserves to be loved.'

All Phoebe wanted was to make Octavio see her. She tried for the glass again, but it was as though an invisible barrier was holding her just far enough away that she couldn't break through.

And then, in that way dreams had, everything changed, and suddenly Octavio was fading before her eyes, slowly losing colour and becoming invisible.

'I could accept dying but for one thing. Leaving my child behind, knowing that he would be alone and how he would miss us. I hoped someone would love him, would hug and hold him and make the hurt better. But no one did. He hurt so much, for so long.'

She could only see his eyes now…jet-black, staring straight ahead. The rest of his body had faded into nothing, leaving the most haunting, awful sense that churned Phoebe's insides.

Then even his eyes disappeared, and Octavio was completely gone…

She woke, screaming, so Octavio woke, too, reaching for her instantly, looking around to ascertain if there was a danger.

'Phoebe?'

'It's—'

Her heart was racing, her body was covered in sweat.

She stared at him, reaching for him, sobbed when her fingers connected with warm flesh. There was no barrier here. Octavio was in their bed, close enough to touch. She wrapped her arms around him and hugged him, listening to his heart again—racing now at the shock of being woken by a scream, as her own was racing from the shock of watching him disappear.

'Are you okay?'

She nodded, her throat thick. She wasn't sure she could speak.

'It was a dream. A terrible dream.'

She felt him stroking her back, seeking to reassure her. All she could think about was the way he'd disappeared before her eyes. And a voice, his mother's voice, though Phoebe had never heard it, pleading with her to love him.

Her throat felt thick. She was caught between the dream and reality, between who they were and what the dream had seemed to push her towards.

Sadness clawed at her insides.

It was a construct of her own pregnancy. An amalgam of her hopes for their babies and a reflection on the things Octavio had endured.

'Would you like to talk about it?'

She instinctively shied away from that. How could she talk about it when she barely understood it? How could she talk about it to Octavio, of all people?

She forced a smile but the effort physically hurt. 'That's okay.' Her voice was hoarse. She cleared her throat. 'It was just a dream.'

Except, it wasn't just a dream. It was a tangible force that prevented her from sleeping, so for once she was awake when Octavio stirred and stepped from their bed a while later. Naked, glorious, but broken. Broken in a way she hadn't fully understood before now. Broken in a way she saw and wanted to fix.

But why?

Why should she?

Would he even want that?

'My nannies taught me to be tough. To rely on no one.'

Was it a lesson that could be unlearned? Would he come to understand that she could be trusted?

Phoebe stared at his back, rigid and strong, and her insides swirled. More importantly, could she trust him? What she'd been through with Christopher had been devastating, but Phoebe had been a grown woman who'd known herself to have been loved by her mother for her most formative years. Octavio had had the rug pulled from under him at a vital age and had then been raised by a man who—from the outside—seemed determined to destroy the young Prince.

'Octavio?' she said his name into the room, as the dawn light softened their surrounds and made everything seem almost coated in gold. He turned, frowning.

'You're awake?'

She nodded.

'Because of the nightmare?'

'In part.' She hesitated. 'Do you need to go straight away?'

His frown was infinitesimal. 'Do you want me to stay?' he asked as he moved back to the bed and sat next to her.

Her stomach was a tumble of nerves. She did. She wanted him to stay desperately, but she was terrified of this conversation. Just as she was about to tell him she was fine, that he could leave, she heard his mother's voice; she saw Octavio disappearing from her and she sat up straighter, reaching for the sheet and folding it under her arms.

'Just for a bit. I need to speak with you.'

But why had the dream devastated her so much? Why had the thought of losing Octavio flooded her with so much pain it had been like a visceral, gaping wound? What could she say to him now? Was she really going to tell him that a version of his mother's ghost had come to her in a dream? It sounded ridiculous. She shook her head. This wasn't about the dream; it was about what he'd told her.

'Octavio.' She put her hand on his thigh. His strong, powerful thigh. All of him was strong, his power was absolute. And yet he'd been emotionally stripped raw as a boy by an adult who'd been trusted to care for him. Her outrage overtook anything else. 'What happened to you, after your parents died…it wasn't okay.'

A muscle jerked in his jaw. 'I've made my peace with it.'

'But have you? Have you really?'

'It was a long time ago, as I said.'

'But isn't it still affecting you?'

His nostrils flared. 'My uncle has no ability to affect me any more.'

'I can see why that's important to you to feel, but he was the one person who could have loved you and shielded you and really cared for you, and instead—'

'Instead he did everything he could to make me miserable. For as long as I was his ward. Yes, I am aware of this. But I came of age more than ten years ago. I dealt with my feelings then. Now all I care about is retaining the power that is my birthright and erasing his damage from my parents' legacy.'

Her heart panged and it was impossible to miss the feeling, nor to misunderstand it.

She didn't want that to be all he cared about.

She wanted him to care about her, too. Not just as the mother of his children, but as a woman. As the woman he'd married, the woman he wanted. She wanted him to more than care for her; she wanted him to love her. If Octavio loved her, would she trust herself to love him back? Would she be willing to risk getting hurt all over again, but so much worse than it had been with Christopher?

Was it even an option?

It wasn't about trusting herself to love. Somewhere along the way, she'd fallen in love. Actual love—the all-consuming, heart-stopping, world-shaking love. She couldn't pinpoint the moment it had happened, but when she looked back, she wondered if even that first night, in the hospital, when she'd stayed with him instead of doing the smart thing and leaving, if there hadn't been a part of her that had somehow been destined to be with him. To love him and to help him accept that love was safe after all. At least, it was with the right person.

Her tongue darted out and licked her lower lip. She stared across at him, her heart in her throat, her whole body on tenterhooks.

'Is that all you wanted to talk about?'

She stared at him, terrified. She loved him. She loved this man who'd told her again and again that their relationship would never be real. She loved a man who was so emotionally closed off because of what he'd endured that she had no idea if she'd ever get through to him, but she knew she had to try.

'No.' The word was almost a groan. She closed her eyes on a wave of nausea. 'Octavio, in my dream, you were in the palace and I couldn't get to you. You were there, staring straight ahead, but you couldn't see me. I kept trying to knock on the glass but I couldn't quite reach it. There was something invisible holding me back. And then you started to disappear in front of my eyes, fading away from me, and I couldn't stop it. I lost you, and it was the worst feeling in the world.'

He frowned, as though he couldn't comprehend what she was saying. 'But I'm right here. It was just a dream.'

'You're missing the point. I thought it was a bad dream, and it was, but maybe it was actually the dream I needed to have to wake me up and make me see with my own eyes what my heart has been telling me all along.'

He was suddenly very still, his features locked in a mask of disciplined coldness. 'And what's that?'

She wanted to bury herself under the sheet; she wanted to run away. But she couldn't. Not after starting this. 'I love you.' Three small words, so simple, but so life-changing, whether they were returned or not. 'I love you,' she repeated. 'I love everything about you. I know what we both agreed this marriage would be, but it's so much more than that. We're going to be parents, a family, and I want to start that with total honesty. Mostly, I want you to know that you are so loved. By me. I love you,' she said, again, when he was silent.

He closed his eyes, his face paling before her eyes. As though it was the worst thing she could have said. As though he had hated hearing it. 'I see.'

'I don't think you do,' she contradicted fiercely. 'I *love you*. All of you. I love who you are, who you've been, what you've done, what you're working towards. I love that you're going to be the father to my children. I love you.'

He stood then, dislodging the hand she'd placed on his thigh. 'With respect, you do not.'

Her heart twisted but she stayed the course. 'I think I know how I feel.'

'You're misinterpreting it. You're seeing sex and reading love. They're not the same thing. I warned you about that.'

'They're not the same thing, but nor are they mutually exclusive. I love you. I love having sex with you. Both things can be true at once.'

'But they're not. This is just about the sex. And maybe a bit about your pregnancy hormones making you feel things—or want things—that would turn this sham of a marriage into something more desirable. You want to believe we're living some kind of fairy tale but that's not what this is. We got trapped by a stupid one-night stand and we've made the best of it.'

She sucked in a sharp breath at his awful, hurtful words. How dare he say that?

'I'm not saying I'm not pleased. I need an heir, and you being pregnant means I will have not one but two, and quickly. This is very good news for me. But I have been clear all along about what you mean to me, what our marriage is to me. This is a means to an end, nothing more.' His nostrils flared. 'You *do not* love me.'

She swallowed hard but her mouth was dry and her tongue would hardly cooperate. He turned towards the wardrobe, disappearing inside of it and returning only moments later dressed in an impeccable suit, looking regal and untouchable. She shivered.

'Don't think about this any more. It's a silly child's fantasy, and you and I both know better than to hope for that.'

He began to walk towards the bedroom door, and she was so angry she would have pitched something after him if there were an object to hand.

'You can say that a million times, it won't change the way I feel, Octavio. I love you!' She shouted the last words, as if by raising the volume of her voice they would permeate his stupid, stubborn head and find their way to his heart.

He slammed the door when he left the suite, and Phoebe fell back against the pillows, tears forming on her lashes.

He felt like a caged predator, a wild beast that had suddenly been locked away, as he went through the day's meetings, scheduled back-to-back, just as he usually liked it. But today, he would have killed for an ounce of breathing room. Just a little freedom to think clearly about Phoebe and her dream, her words, particularly three little words she'd said again and again. Only the moment he allowed his mind to turn to her, to recollect her face as she'd said those words, everything in his body had come to a catastrophic stall. It was as if his blood ceased pumping, his heart ceased working, his lungs stopped inflating, his cells froze. Every part of him rejected every part of what she'd said. He couldn't let her do this to him. He couldn't let her make him think and feel...feel anything.

It just wasn't what they were, and it sure as hell wasn't what he wanted.

But was that the truth?

Hadn't there been a small part of him, a part that Octavio had immediately tamped down, that had heard her words as one might see a perfect ray of light piercing thick, grey clouds? Hadn't there been a part of him— the part that his childhood had all but destroyed—that had wanted to revive and delight in what she was offering him?

He dropped his head forward on a rush of disbelief and determination. There was no way he would be so stupid as to let that part of him grow, however. Octavio knew what he wanted in life, he knew how to get it, and most importantly, he knew what Phoebe and his marriage were. This wasn't about love.

It wasn't about anything personal.

But what if it is? That niggling voice pushed, harder and with more determination. What if, despite all his efforts, something about Phoebe had got under his skin, too?

He tried to follow that thought through to its conclusion, imagined the impact that would have on their marriage and the way their relationship would change. He imagined the power she would have over him, the destructive ability to *hurt* him, and he knew it just wasn't possible. To love someone was to trust them in a way that Octavio had learned never to trust. It would make him vulnerable, and Octavio had to be strong—for himself and the sake of his country.

Phoebe didn't love him. She couldn't. She had been caught up in a fantasy, because of their marriage and the pregnancy, but she'd see and accept the limitations of what they were again soon. Wouldn't she?

Thoughts like this chased themselves around and around his head all day, and as the day drew on, the thought of returning to his apartment, and to Phoebe, kept having the same impact on him. He didn't want to see her; he didn't want to risk having more of the conversation she'd started that morning. He couldn't hear her say those words again, knowing that he'd never return them. Even if he wanted to. Which he didn't.

He was gripped by a need for space and time, by a need to run away. And though it was a childish urge to surrender to, as the afternoon fell, he called for his private secretary. 'I'm going to the embassy in Spain for a night or two.' He took a deep breath, imagined how Phoebe would feel when she realised that he was hiding from her.

Coward, his inner voice growled. *Be man enough to face her.*

But then he saw Phoebe's face in his mind, and everything inside him began to twist with panic. He had to get away. 'There's something I want to work on there. Would you have someone let Her Majesty know?'

With a curt nod, the aide was dismissed and Octavio was able to breathe a little more clearly.

She caught him as he was on his way to the helipad and her temper was such that she clearly didn't notice the guards standing watch just across from them.

'You're running away? Are you kidding me?'

His eyes narrowed, a muscle jerking in his jaw. He hadn't wanted to see her again; he hadn't been prepared for this. Clearly his message had reached her prematurely; he'd planned to be in the air before it was delivered. 'I beg your pardon?'

'You can beg all you bloody want. You won't get it. I never had you pegged as a coward, Octavio.'

He glared back at her, his nostrils flaring. 'You have no right to speak to me like that.'

She flinched. 'Don't talk to me like I'm a stranger.'

'You are acting like one. What the hell has got into you?'

'You're running away.' She jabbed a finger against his chest. 'Because you're scared to finish the conversation we started this morning.'

He turned towards the guards and dismissed them with a gesture. Alone in the corridor, just a flight of stairs from the rooftop, he turned back to her. 'That conversation is already finished as far as I'm concerned.'

'You think?' She folded her arms with a huff of something like disdain. 'You think you can just walk out on a woman who's baring her soul to you?'

'You are letting your hormones control you. This will pass.'

'Don't you dare do that. Don't gaslight me. I know what I feel and I know what I want.'

He drew himself to his full height, his expression ominous. 'Unfortunately, so do I.'

'And it's not me?'

'It's this marriage, with you, and it's these babies, but it is not love, it is none of the things you spoke of this morning.'

'Wow.' She blinked quickly, her body trembling slightly. With anger? 'So you're saying you don't love me?'

He stared at her for several long beats. 'We've discussed this.'

'I need to hear it. Say the words.'

But it was a bridge too far. Octavio knew what was in his heart, he was pretty sure he knew what was in hers, too. This wasn't love, for either of them. He wasn't a complete bastard though. He had no interest in saying things that were bound to hurt her.

'I've said how I feel.'

'No, you haven't. Not directly. So say it,' she challenged, shoulders squared.

He focused hard on her face, willing her to see into his soul, to understand that he would never love anyone. It just wasn't a part of his capabilities any more. It was no deficiency of hers; it was just how Octavio was. As he'd been bred to be, after his parents' death. 'I have no wish to hurt you.'

She flinched.

'I have always been clear about that.'

'Yes, you have. Calculatedly so.'

'You say that as if it's a bad thing.'

Her lips trembled a little. He felt the bones in his body grow tight and painful. He looked away, dragging a hand through his hair. 'I'm not running away,' he said quietly. 'But we both need some space from this. In a few days, you'll realise how stupid it all is.'

She flinched again. 'Loving someone isn't stupid.'

'Did you love Christopher?'

Her face paled. 'Don't bring him into this.'

'Why not? You were wrong about him. How do you know you're not wrong about me?'

'Because you're a completely different person. Don't you think I've thought of that? Don't you think I've been fighting with myself about that—you, him, my flawed judgement—this whole time? But you are *not* him, just like you've said. You are his exact opposite in every way. Loving you is not a mistake, and it's not based on a lie.'

'Maybe it is. Maybe I've been lying to you without realising it. Because if you're standing there expecting me to be able to say that I love you, then you've totally misunderstood who I am and what I want in life. And how can you be in love with me, if that's the case? How can you love someone you don't know?' He felt as though he'd landed the winning shot. His words made so much sense, all the sense in the world, so he breathed out, relieved that he'd offered an argument that would surely sway her.

He took a step backwards, preparing to escape, but as he turned his back, she said, sadly, softly, 'Or what if I know you better than you know yourself? What if I can see what you're not capable of seeing? What if I love you so much that I understand how hard it is for you to admit you love me back, but I'm willing to wait? What about that, Tavi?'

He didn't want to hear that. He didn't want to hear it and take it on board, and so he kept walking, shoulders squared, face set in a mould of determination. It was only as the helicopter took off that he dropped his head forward and admitted to himself that he had the strangest sense his world was crumbling down around him again, in almost the same way it had when his parents had died.

CHAPTER FOURTEEN

THE HELICOPTER LIFTED and the palace began to look small. Tiny, really. A place that held so many memories for Octavio, so many memories of his life. His time with his parents and Rodrigo, times of happiness and care, of love and warmth. Times that he hated to think back to, despite their warmth, because of how badly they contrasted with what came next.

The loss, the grief, the despair. The feeling of being completely uprooted from everything and everyone he'd ever known. The conclusion he'd reached at that point, that there were no guarantees in life. That the only thing he would ever be able to control was himself, his interactions with people and who he let near him.

And so he'd been careful.

He'd been careful in terms of who he surrounded himself with, he was careful with his time, attention, focus, relationships. His boundaries and rules. He was careful *all the time.* And it was exhausting. But what was exhaustion when the alternative was allowing someone else to hold the controls to your life and happiness?

So he was still careful, even with Phoebe, which was precisely how he knew he didn't love her. He didn't *need* her. He'd be fine without her. The whole idea of her loving him was a construct, some kind of romantic notion dreamed up because of the pregnancy. Just like he'd said to her. She was hormonal. Fanciful. Just plain wrong.

He dropped his head forward as the air whooshed out of his lungs.

Had he actually said that to her?

The morning's conversation came rushing back to him, the conversation he'd been avoiding remembering all day. He could see now how hurtful he'd been. He'd chosen words almost as if deliberately aiming to wound her, to insult her intelligence and—what had she called it?—gaslight her. He'd been so afraid of what she was saying, of the picture she was painting, of even the merest possibility that he might not have been able to maintain the control he fought so hard for, that he'd responded to her brave confession by shutting it down in the most direct way possible. Because he hadn't wanted to hear it.

He'd panicked.

The city was now a blanket of lights, and yet he could still pick out the landmarks, the layout, the streets and parks he knew so well and was now in command of.

He loved this place. He loved his people. He loved the honour that had been bestowed upon him, to be King of this ancient Mediterranean country. There he was able to love without restraint, because countries could not hurt people. Countries could not wound.

Was he so afraid of Phoebe hurting him?

No.

It wasn't that. It was a deeper fear: that he might lose her. That he might lose not just her, but one day, her love. That she might turn away from him? That he didn't deserve her. Just as all those nannies and his uncle Mauricio had made him feel, all his life.

He was afraid. Terrified.

And hadn't he known that all along? From his first meeting with Phoebe, hadn't he sensed something within her that was different and unusual, something that threatened not just his equilibrium but the very safe, very ordered lines he lived within? The intensity of his need for her—not just physically, he conceded now, but in every way—had overtaken his senses from that first meeting. When he hadn't been with her, he'd craved her. He had fought that, tooth and nail, pretending that he was only proposing because of her pregnancy, pretending that their marriage was the last thing he personally wanted, when wasn't the opposite true? He'd wanted *Phoebe*. Not as the mother to his heirs, but for herself. Her wonderful, beautiful self.

But he'd run from that. He'd been running from it for as long as he'd known her, fighting himself and what she was coming to mean to him, because of the survival skills he'd developed to cope with the emotional abuse he'd endured every day since his parents' death, until finally, as an adult, he could liberate himself from that oppression.

He sat up a little straighter, a strange heady rush of adrenaline pumping through him.

He knew his upbringing had been wrong and cruel. He knew that he'd been deliberately worn down, and he thought that had made him strong. Despite their attempts, he'd grown up and shown them all: no one could break him.

No one could hurt him.

But what if they were hurting him still? What if their efforts to whittle away his joy had long, snaking tendrils, creeping into his life still, stopping him from seeing what was right in front of him? What could be in front of him for all time, if he played his cards right and was very, very lucky? It was a risk—but wasn't everything? Wasn't getting in this helicopter a risk? A plane?

He was almost breathless when he reached for his headset and slipped it in place, allowing him to communicate directly with the pilot. 'Take us back to the palace. Immediately.'

Phoebe had stayed in the corridor until the sound of the rotor blades had disappeared and then she'd begun to walk away. Slowly. Each step felt like she was wading through mud, and that had nothing to do with her growing stomach.

It hurt.

Everything hurt.

The last thing she'd called after him was that she was willing to wait for him to wake up and realise how he felt about her. But was she really? Could she do that? Could she live this life, by his side, raising his babies, knowing he might never love her back?

Or worse—that he might love her but have no idea how to admit it?

She groaned, pressing her fingers to her forehead. She was lost, wandering aimlessly through the palace, staring at ancient art, flowers, guards' faces, seeing nothing, because her whole heart and mind were taken up thinking about Octavio and how much she wanted him to see what they were. She wanted him to trust this, but he wouldn't. She knew how stubbornly he wanted to hold to his habits of not letting anyone in, and she could understand why. Hearing about the way he'd been treated after his parents' death only hardened her resolve to be brave: to admit she loved him and put herself on the line again. Just like with Christopher.

But nothing like it, at the same time.

She had never loved Christopher. She could see that now. She'd needed him in the sense of the time they'd met—even years after her mother's death she had still been floundering and miserable. He'd filled a void for her and distracted her from the worst of her grief. She'd become used to him and had liked spending time with him. Theirs had been a relationship of natural progression, at least for Phoebe. She'd liked him, therefore she'd thought it logical that after a certain amount of time she might love him. And a little time after that, she'd realised that the sensible thing to do was to get married and start a family. It had all been a series of steps, a path she'd started on and just kept following because...why not?

It wasn't like that with Octavio.

She needed him because of who he was. She hadn't been able to get him out of her head from the very beginning because he'd started to exist in her blood. Meeting him had been the striking of a match and the next minute, she'd been in the middle of a full-blown wildfire. The heat was scorching, her love for him would not end. She stopped walking and closed her eyes.

When she opened them, she glanced around, a little lost. Where was she? This part of the palace was no longer familiar. She pushed through a door, nodding once at the guard outside, finding herself in a room that was very old, very formal and very beautiful. If somewhat intimidating.

She took a seat by the unlit fireplace and stared at it, wondering when the aching in her heart would stop.

He had no idea why she'd ended up in the cigar room, of all places, but according to his guards, that's where his wife had gone after he'd left. His wife. The words took on a whole new significance now. Octavio jogged through the corridors, thinking with a small smile of what his mother would have said. She had scolded him when he'd run like this as a child, delighting in the never-ending expanses of corridors, perfect to treat like a sports stadium when he was bored. She'd scolded him but always with a slight smile in place, as though she understood that a fire was in his soul, and this was the only way to put it out.

He ran faster, until his lungs hurt, and as he rounded the corner of the corridor that housed the cigar room, a guard, who had perhaps been feeling the effects of a long day at his post and was almost asleep on his feet, reacted with a look of shock to see the King come sprinting past him.

'Your Majesty,' the guard said in surprise.

Octavio didn't stop.

Only when he approached the door he wanted did he slow down to allow air to fill his lungs so that he would be capable of speech. The guard at the door gave him a quizzical look and then nodded once.

'Her Majesty has not left.'

'Excellent. See that we are not disturbed.'

'Yes, sir.'

Octavio hesitated at the door a moment, but he'd come

this far and wasn't going to let a little something like last-minute nerves get in the way. He knocked on the door perfunctorily and then pushed it open, his gut twisting at the sight of Phoebe. His wife. His pregnant wife. His beautiful, kind, selfless, pregnant wife, who had also suffered so much in her life and deserved better than to ever feel like this. For the woman in the chair across the room was a study in grief and despair, and he had done that to her.

He closed the door and crossed the room, startling her out of her reverie just as he had the guard.

'Octavio!' Her eyes widened, her pinched features did their best to rearrange themselves and hide the sadness she was feeling. 'What are you doing here?' She wiped her hands over her skirt. 'I thought you were flying somewhere or other.'

'I was,' he admitted. 'I got up there and looked down at the palace and thought of you and realised that this, here, is exactly where I want to be. So I came back. I came home.'

Home. Yes. That's what Phoebe made him feel—that he had a home. And it wasn't about the palace, but rather wherever she was. It had been so long since he'd felt anything like that. It was a revelation to Octavio, but the revelations kept coming.

'Oh.' But she was uncertain and unsure. Could he blame her? She'd put herself out on a limb for him, not once but twice. He thought of how brave she'd been to admit her feelings even to herself, but then to confess them to him that morning and chase him down this afternoon. She had been brave where he'd been determined to fight and hide.

'I'm sorry,' he said, because it felt important to admit that. He'd messed up. He knew it, he wanted her to know it, too.

'It's fine. You were right. You were honest with me from the beginning. I let my own wishes get in the way of reality. I wanted this to be a real marriage. I wanted us to love each other and to be having a baby out of love. Maybe that's because I never saw that with my parents and always craved the ideal of a happy family. For whatever reason, I imagined something that wasn't there. You don't have to apologise for not being as stupid as I am.'

'You're not stupid,' he responded indignantly. But his gears were churning, his mind spinning. 'Are you saying you were wrong about your feelings?' And did that matter? Having realised how he felt, wasn't it his job to be brave and admit that he loved her, even if she took back what she'd said earlier?

'I'm saying I shouldn't have brought any of this up. I wanted you to know how loved you are, but you don't need that. You don't want it. I was being selfish, saying what I wanted to say without respecting that it's the last thing you wanted to hear.'

'That's just not the case, Phoebe. You are never selfish, and it's certainly not selfish to tell someone you love them.'

'With you, it is. So I'm the one who's sorry.'

'Stop. Don't do that.' His voice was raw and he realised then how much she was hurting him—without realising it. He pressed a finger to her lips, needing her to stop winding back everything she'd said. He couldn't bear it. 'Listen to me. I don't know what you're saying and what it means. Perhaps you don't feel as you thought you did, or you have changed your mind. Regardless, I need to tell you what I realised, as the helicopter lifted up and took me in the opposite direction of you.'

She blinked across at him, her eyes so lovely and bewitching. 'What?' The word was whispered against his finger, her breath warm. He closed his eyes on a predictable wave of desire. This was not the time to let their chemistry run the show.

'You're where I want to be.' It sounded so simple, and maybe it was. 'You are my home,' he said, because that was the best way to describe it. 'And you have my heart.'

Her own heart was racing so hard she could barely hear him over the gushing in her ears. She heard his words and she was sure she understood them, but what if she was wrong? She needed to be very, very clear before she reacted, because so much was riding on this conversation. The nature of their marriage hung in the balance—because she knew one thing for sure. She couldn't keep living with him, sleeping with him, when she loved and he did not reciprocate those feelings.

'You are my wife,' he said, but in a way that imbued the word with an almost mythical quality. 'The only wife I would ever choose or want. You are the wife I want to live with and love for the rest of my days, to have by my side at all times—good and bad. You are the person I want to raise a family with, hold hands with as the sun sets, share meals with, talk to until our voices are raspy, wake up next to, reach out for in the middle of the night. You are everything I have ever wanted and thought so far out of my reach.'

She gasped, her heart trembling now.

'I realised, as I flew away from you, how conditioned I had been to believe I didn't deserve this. That no one would ever love me. That's why I fought you this morning, and again just now. How could anyone love me? But particularly, how could *you*? You are so perfect— an angel, here amongst men—there was no way I could believe you were actually saying these things. No way I could trust your love to be true.'

'It is true,' she said emphatically, sharply, furious at what those awful nannies had done to him, at the behavioural programming his uncle had employed. 'I love you and you are so, so worthy of that love, my darling Tavi. My husband.' And when she said the word, it was just as imbued with meaning as Octavio had made the word *wife* seem—so much more than a title or a statement of fact. It was everything. A statement of the truth in her heart and the gift she wanted to make of it for him. She caught his face with her hands, holding him steady so she could look at him—but more importantly, so that he could look at her and really see her.

'In the dream I had, you couldn't see me. I was calling to you, and I just couldn't reach you, couldn't make you see me nor hear me. It was a nightmare.'

'I see you now. I see what I have, what I have been blessed with.'

'What *I* have been blessed with,' she said with a shake of her head. 'You don't understand—I came to Castilona looking for my father. Needing family and connection, after my mum and after Christopher. I didn't want to feel like this piece of meaningless flotsam any more, uprooted and disconnected. I didn't want to be alone any more, even when I was also terrified of making the same mistakes all over again. But I had no idea that in coming here I would meet *you*, my other half, and that we would on that very first night conceive two babies who would bind us for ever.' A tear ran down her cheek. He lifted a hand and gently wiped it away.

'You came to Castilona looking for family, and you found it,' he said, dropping his forehead to hers. 'And we will still try to find your father, *querida*, to complete the puzzle for you. But in the meantime, you are here, and you are mine, as I am yours.'

She nodded, with a levity in her heart because she knew, without a shadow of doubt, that he spoke the absolute truth. This was their destiny, and their fate, and they'd found their way to it despite everything they'd been through. Or perhaps because of it. Despite their determined efforts to avoid anything like love, perhaps their experiences had made them both recognise how special their connection was even before they were ready to admit it. Phoebe couldn't analyse it more deeply than that, in the moment, but she was aware, as their lips brushed and held, that something almost magical had happened between them, and she would never stop feeling grateful and glad.

Except, as time passed and Phoebe fully stepped into a life with King Octavio—a life in which each knew how loved and valued they were and what a true partnership they'd formed—she found her mind turning to the key points of their relationship, analysing it, and her sense of wonderment only grew and grew. So much so, that one night, when they were standing on a private terrace of the palace, Octavio's arm wrapped around Phoebe as

they stared up at the starlit sky, Phoebe admitted something that she hadn't fully comprehended herself yet.

'That night we met,' she started slowly. 'Do you ever
think it seemed almost beyond our control?'

He glanced down at her, frowning a little.

'That sounds vague,' she admitted, laughing softly.
'It's just…' She searched for the right words. 'I told you
that my mother was a cleaner in a hospital, and that's
part of the reason I took the job at the *clínica*, but lately
I've been feeling like it was more than that. Like maybe
somehow, on some level, she was pushing me there. Towards you.'

He didn't dismiss it. Instead, he nodded, thoughtfully.
'The night I met you, I was thinking of my own mother.
She would say to me, whenever she travelled, *"We'll always have the stars."* It was her way of reminding me
that no matter where we were, if we were separated, we
could both look out at the sky and see the stars and know
we were thinking of each other. But that night, there were
no stars. When I needed her most, in my grief, I felt only
her absence. I felt alone. And then, there you were, right
when I needed you.'

Phoebe's smile was wobbly. 'There's one more thing
I haven't told you.'

He waited for her to speak.

'That dream I had.' She shuddered even now, remembering it. 'Your mother was in it. Well, not your mother,
but her voice, telling me that her deepest hope was that
you would be loved. That you would understand you
were worthy of love.'

In response to that he closed his eyes as though his
feelings were too deep.

'It made me realise my feelings—and how selfish I was, in not being honest with you. Your mother was right—you are so worthy of love, and as soon as I understood how much I loved you, I knew that my own fear of making a mistake like I had with Christopher wasn't a good enough reason not to tell you how I felt.' She shook her head. 'It was a terrible dream, but I'm so glad I had it.'

'A terrible dream with a happy ending,' he agreed, placing a hand on her stomach. The babies kicked and they both smiled. The stars shone down on them and Phoebe felt a warm, perfect sense of completion. She knew, without a shadow of a doubt, that she was right where she was meant to be.

EPILOGUE

IN THE END, they learned the truth of Phoebe's father quite by accident. Or perhaps it was yet another example of the hand of fate exerting itself over their lives, driving them towards a future that was truly and utterly complete.

Some years after they'd reached out and grabbed their happiness with both hands, Octavio was meeting with a group of advisors and politicians. He had worked tirelessly to restore the country to a state of good government, and these men were amongst his most trusted team members. Some of them had even served in his parents' government and parliament.

One in particular, he found he relied on quite heavily, in terms of counsel and advice, a man whose wisdom always seemed to be just what he needed to hear in the moment. But there was something else about the man that held Octavio's attention, something familiar that he just couldn't place. It was at the end of the meeting, when Rafael Herrera was packing up to leave, and Octavio couldn't help but notice a certain efficiency to the man's movement that was almost graceful. He felt a frisson of something spark in his belly.

'Would you stay a moment?' he asked, his voice slightly hoarse, his heart racing with the possibility...

but surely it was extremely unlikely. The name was not the same, and he'd known this man for years. But perhaps Rafael might have a relation, a brother, who shared the same name as Phoebe's father? Or perhaps he was being fanciful; seeing ghosts out of a desperate need to help his wife. Though she was happier than he'd ever known another human to be, at times, he caught her looking into space and frowning and he'd understood where her thoughts had taken her.

'Of course, Your Majesty.'

'Please, call me Octavio,' he invited, because this was going to be a very personal conversation. 'I wanted to ask you something—something quite unusual.'

'Anything, of course.'

He was not going to just come out and say it though. 'Have you ever been to New Zealand, Rafael?'

The other man looked a little taken aback. 'Is there a reason you ask, sir?'

'You know my wife is from there.'

'Yes, naturally.'

Octavio frowned. Rafael Herrera knew the Queen was from New Zealand and he had undoubtedly seen pictures of her. If there was a similarity between them, wouldn't he have noticed it himself? Then again, according to Phoebe, her father had never known she'd even been conceived. It was a stretch to think he might have been able to make the connection without knowing one existed.

'For some time, she has been looking for her biological father. All she had was his name and the fact that he was from Castilona. Once, we thought we were close—a man was found matching the physical description, name and approximate age, but he had never been to New Zealand.'

Rafael was standing very still, and Octavio's skin lifted in goose bumps all over.

'What is her father's name?' he asked with urgency.

'Carlos Guttierez.'

'I need—I'm—' Rafael looked around, quite helpless. Octavio moved quickly, grabbing a seat and placing it behind the older man.

'Sit,' he urged.

He collapsed into the chair, dropping his face into his hands.

'And her mother's name?'

'Jennifer James.'

'Jenny,' he whispered, groaning. 'Dear God, Jenny.' He looked up at Octavio, his eyes huge. 'I didn't know.'

'Why don't you start at the beginning, and if it checks out, I will bring this to my wife.'

He found her in the rose garden, a picture of serenity, surrounded by their children, books and blocks, and his heart tightened. Silently he signalled for the nanny to take over—a nanny they had screened and found to be a paragon of love and kindness, just the sort of person one would wish to care for their children when busy with official engagements.

'*Querida?* We need to speak.' He drew her to a private part of the garden and they sat together on a white timber bench.

'Back then,' Octavio explained carefully, after the initial shocking announcement had been made, 'your father did not work as a diplomat—he was a spy, involved in some very dangerous missions. He was holidaying in New Zealand and when he travelled, he always did so under a different identity. His work was very dangerous, and it didn't enter his mind that it would cause a problem for your mother. He says they were careful— she was on the pill, they used protection, he had no reason to think there was even the slightest chance you had been conceived.'

Tears filled her eyes. 'I cannot believe this. And you say you *know* him?'

'I've worked with him for years,' Octavio admitted. 'My parents knew him, *querida*.'

Phoebe gasped.

'A couple of years after returning from New Zealand, he stopped his work as an operative and joined the parliament. He quit once my parents died and Mauricio became King and then returned shortly before my coronation. He is on a committee of advisors I meet with regularly, and I have no doubt, my darling love, that he is your father.'

Tears ran down her cheeks.

'He is very upset,' Octavio admitted. 'He intentionally left no way for your mother to contact him, though he asked me to tell you that, had his life been different, he might have left everything behind to be with her. He says that though their affair was brief, he's never forgotten her.' Octavio hesitated. 'He is married now, though, and has children from that marriage.'

Phoebe blanched, and then squealed. 'You mean I have *siblings*?'

Octavio's relief was immense. He wasn't sure what he'd expected, but her delight in this was more than he'd hoped. 'Yes, darling. Two sisters and a brother, and though Rafael and I agree you must decide how you'd like to proceed, he asked me to let you know that he couldn't wait to meet you, and that he knows his wife and children will feel the same way.'

'I can't believe it, Octavio. We have *family*. Extended family. And a family who can tell us about my mother and about your parents. Can you believe we are really this blessed?'

He stood then, wrapping his arms around her. 'I can, my darling. I really, really can.'

And they were blessed, and a great blessing indeed to the country of Castilona. Before this happy, happy conclusion to their story though, there was a hardship for the royal couple, one that they navigated, side by side, and with the help of cousin Xiomara. Like all expectant parents, every prenatal appointment was a time of deeply mixed emotion. Happiness and excitement, mixed with fear and adrenaline, because it was so easy to believe that something might go wrong.

Phoebe though had become somewhat complacent. After all, these babies were so 'meant to be,' they'd been conceived almost as if willed into existence by fate and angels.

So when she lay on the bed for her twenty-week ultrasound, her stomach covered in goo, the last thing she expected was to see lines of concern on the obstetrician's face, and the announcement that he would need to consult with a colleague.

The director of the *clínica*, Lola Garcia, attempted to distract them, but it was an impossible task. All Phoebe could think about was the unmistakable signs of worry on the doctor's features, and her whole stomach had turned into a tangle of knots.

After receiving the news that parents dread, that indeed, there were medical complications with their pregnancy, Octavio's first call was to Xiomara. His cousin was his closest ally, aside from his wife, the one person he could rely on, always, to have his back.

'Help me, Xiomara. Help me. I'll do whatever it takes...'

'And so will I, Tavi. Leave it with me. Everything's going to be okay. I promise.'

And Xiomara left Castilona with that promise heavy in her mind. Everything would be okay, because she'd damn well make sure of it...

* * * * *

If Twins for his Majesty *left you wanting more, then don't miss the next instalment in the Royally Tempted trilogy, coming soon!*

And why not explore these other stories from Clare Connelly?

Contracted and Claimed by the Boss
His Runaway Royal
Pregnant Before the Proposal
Unwanted Royal Wife
Billion-Dollar Secret Between Them

Available now!

   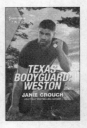